Sticky Notes

Sticky Notes

Dianne Touchell

A YEARLING BOOK

Text copyright © 2014 by Dianne Touchell
Cover art copyright © 2018 by Oriol Vidal

All rights reserved. Published in the United States by Yearling, an imprint of Random House Children's Books, a division of Penguin Random House LLC, New York. Originally published in paperback as *Forgetting Foster* by Allen & Unwin, Crows Nest, Australia, in 2016, and subsequently published in hardcover in the United States by Delacorte Press, an imprint of Random House Children's Books, a division of Penguin Random House LLC, New York, in 2018.

Yearling and the jumping horse design are registered trademarks of Penguin Random House LLC.

Visit us on the Web! rhcbooks.com

Educators and librarians, for a variety of teaching tools, visit us at RHTeachersLibrarians.com

The Library of Congress has cataloged the hardcover edition of this work as follows:
Names: Touchell, Dianne, author.
Title: Sticky notes / Dianne Touchell.
Description: First American edition. | New York: Delacorte Press, [2018] | "Originally published in paperback by Allen & Unwin, Crows Nest, Australia in 2016"—Title page verso. | Summary: Seven-year-old Foster has always been close to his father, but now his father is changing and forgetting things, Mum is tired and grumpy, and Foster feels invisible.
Identifiers: LCCN 2016059412 | ISBN 978-1-5247-6548-4 (hc) | ISBN 978-1-5247-6549-1 (glb) | ISBN 978-1-5247-6550-7 (ebook)
Subjects: | CYAC: Alzheimer's disease—Fiction. | Fathers and sons—Fiction. | Memory—Fiction. | Family problems—Fiction.
Classification: LCC PZ7.T647152 St 2018 | DDC [Fic]—dc23

ISBN 978-1-5247-6551-4 (pbk.)

Printed in the United States of America

10 9 8 7 6 5 4 3 2 1

First Yearling Edition 2019

For William George Touchell

Foster smelled it first. A bitter smell like microwave popcorn popped too long. Except Dad wasn't making popcorn. Dad was making bacon sandwiches.

Foster walked into the kitchen. He could see blue flames licking the sides of the pan; the shiny white enamel blackening; and long, sooty fingers crawling toward the lip. A soupy gloom of darkening smoke rolled up and up until it hit the range hood like a solid mass and spilled into the space above Foster's head. It formed clouds he could taste.

"Dad?"

Dad wasn't in the kitchen. You weren't supposed to leave pans on the stove unattended. That's what Mom always said.

"Dad!"

Foster wasn't allowed to touch the stove. He knew how to turn it off, but he didn't want to get in trouble. He took a couple of steps forward, arced himself up on his tippy-toes, and was suddenly and shockingly backhanded by the whooshing heat of the oil in the pan catching fire. Foster ran from the room as the smoke morphed into a pillar of bright orange.

"Dad!"

Foster ran down the hall, instinctively slapping doors ajar, until he got to the last room on the left. Dad was standing at the side of his and Mom's bed sorting socks from the clean laundry pile. He wasn't doing a very good job.

"Dad! Bacon!" Foster pulled at his dad's arm, the smell of smoke indistinguishable from the stinging choke of his panic. It was the smoke alarm that yanked Dad out of his sock daze. He ran to the kitchen, Foster immediately behind him. Foster pressed himself against the pantry door, the relentless squawk of the smoke alarm pulling his breath tighter and faster. Dad clamped the lid on the pan and threw it in the sink. He grabbed a tea towel and started flapping it about wildly, throwing open the kitchen window with such force that it skidded out of the track and cracked as it landed against the frame. Foster slid down the pantry door onto the kitchen floor and squished his ears with his fists. The smoke alarm kept going and going until Dad finally silenced it by stabbing it with a broom handle. Then he slid down to the floor next to Foster.

The wall was black. There were some little blisters in the paint and mucky grease skid marks down the front of the stove and cabinets. The smoke alarm dangled from the ceiling, and splinters of plastic were littered around the discarded broom like flower petals. Foster held Dad's hand, and their breathing gradually slowed together.

"Mom's going to be mad," Foster said.

He could no longer remember the first thing his father forgot. It came on slowly, his dad's forgetting. Like a spider building its web in a doorway. For a while Foster could walk straight through it. He felt it cling to him each time he broke it down, each time he picked the broken bits of it off his face. But then it would reappear in the same place—so fine it was impossible to see unless his eyes were trained on its exact position. Eventually it was like a veil, this forgetting. He could no longer break it; he could only part it to gain a quick peek of his dad on the other side of his lost stories.

His name was Foster Hirum Wylie Sumner, and he was ten years old. His dad told stories. Lots of them. At night before bed, while Foster was brushing his teeth, at the kitchen table, in the car. His dad told stories as if they were real, and long after Foster grew to realize they were just stories, he still craved them. He often asked for his favorite ones to be repeated.

"There are stories in everything," his dad told him. "They are all around you, waiting to be discovered. You just have to look for them."

On story day at school, when moms and dads were invited to come to class to read aloud, it was always his dad who came, even though he had a suit job. Hardly any dads came. It was mostly moms in jeans. But his dad would come from work in the middle of the day carrying a briefcase with a lock that popped like a bad knuckle, and inside would be Foster's favorite books from home. Sometimes his dad would just make a story up on the spot, and even with no pictures everyone was still and quiet, his dad's voice dusting the room like bow rosin, rising and falling to the rhythm of battle cries, dragons, and triumphant heroes. He would walk around the room while he spoke, using his hands and eyes as punctuation, circumnavigating the clusters of desks while boys' faces followed like awestruck marionettes. His dad would always kiss him goodbye afterward. Foster wasn't embarrassed. His dad held more authority in that classroom than the teacher, Mr. Ballantyne, for the brief time he was there. He would shake Mr. Ballantyne's hand before he left, and all the boys would clap. Foster thought he would burst with the pride of it.

Foster's dad encouraged Foster to tell his own stories. "Tell stories to whoever will listen, and then listen to theirs," he would say. Foster liked to tell stories about knights on great quests who would battle bad guys and save ladies, because he knew they were his dad's favorites. Sometimes they would tell a story in tandem. His dad would stop midsentence and look at Foster with his eyebrows knitted and a pressed-lip smile, and Foster would know it was his turn to tell the next bit. He saw this as great trust. Sometimes his mom would listen and laugh at the funny parts and gasp at the scary parts, but when they asked her to join in, she'd say she didn't want to spoil the story.

Foster lived inside his head a lot. His dad said this was a good thing, because there was so much to see there. His mom wanted him to join the local soccer team or something.

"Know thyself," Dad said.

"What's that mean, Dad? Mom talks about her thighs a lot and she thinks I should play soccer."

His dad's laugh was always astonishing, especially when unexpected. He could crack a hole in the air with the bigness of it. It trailed off into snorty giggles before he said, "What?"

"Heard her on the phone," Foster said. "She's on another diet."

"Excuse me," Mom said. "I'm right here."

"Maybe you should play soccer, Mom."

"Knowing *thyself*," Dad continued, chuckling, "is about being happy inside your own head. It means not letting other people tell you what stories are right and what stories are wrong. And it's a wise saying that extends to dieting." Dad leaned across and curled a wisp of Mom's hair behind her ear.

Foster was pretty sure he knew himself relatively well. He liked books and toy soldiers and tadpole hunting and the beach. He liked going to school. He liked the routine—the unremarkable sameness of school days with lessons and bells and his best friend, Blinky, to eat lunch with. There were things he didn't like. He didn't like asparagus or the smell of dog food or prickly grass under his bare feet. He knew these things as surely as he knew the day his mom had put fresh sheets on his bed and the moment his dad had a new story to tell: just by feel. He was unprepared for how much a change in someone else could wilt the pieces of himself he thought he knew best.

Foster sometimes forgot things—mostly at school, when he was supposed to be remembering. When remembering mattered most. But he forgot things other times too. Sometimes he forgot to flush the toilet or hang his towel up after a bath. Twice he'd forgotten to return a library book on time. It never bothered him when he forgot things, because the things eventually came back, or someone would remind him. His dad called it having a hole in his head.

"Got a hole in your head today, Fossie? Better go find those library books."

Everyone had a hole in their head sometimes. Foster had thought it would stay the same size, though, not become bigger and bigger until even a reminder could no longer nudge the forgotten thing back into place.

So it began as only a little worry when his dad started to forget things. Foster wanted to ask him about it, but he wasn't sure what to say. And once in a while there would be a small return of the storyteller, just for a moment, in the car or in the bath, and Foster would think he was being silly and the forgetting had gone away for good.

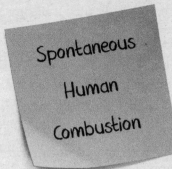

Spontaneous

Human

Combustion

Rumor had it that his grandma was the victim of spontaneous human combustion. Apparently, a little fire had started somewhere inside her while she was sitting alone, crocheting squares to be stitched together to make a blanket. It must have been a little fire initially, because if she'd gone up like a torch, she would have taken the whole house with her. She didn't, which his dad said was just as well because it was the only asset she had. So this little fire started and ate away at her with a gentle fierceness, melting her into her mattress and leaving behind one foot still immaculately tied into a brown lace-up oxford shoe.

Foster watched his own limbs carefully after that, and even sniffed himself occasionally to make sure there were no tendrils of invisible smoke curling from his pores. He asked his dad why his grandma didn't have time to beat herself out. His dad speculated that the fire was somehow magical and impermeable to the quenching effect of smothering like a normal fire.

Grandma had, after all, kept dragons at the bottom of the garden, and fairies lived in their scale-creviced hides like pretty fleas. His dad said the fireflies he sometimes saw weaving about the apple blossoms were actually fairies braiding the eyelashes of the dragons so that when they yawned, the ribbons of flame that escaped their mouths wouldn't set their lashes on fire. So perhaps, his dad said, one of the dragons that sat at the end of Grandma's bed at night, protecting her from thieves and bad dreams, had sneezed and accidentally set her alight. It would have been very quick, like one of those pinwheel fireworks he loved so much. Grandma would have spun and spun, faster and faster, and all the colors of her soul would have flown to the magical place where dragons rest and fairies weave.

"Why was there a foot left behind?" Foster asked.

"She was spinning so fast that it just flew off," his dad replied. "You don't need two feet when you've earned wings."

"Stop it, Malcolm," his mom said. "You know she was smoking in bed."

Foster felt bad when his grandma died. He'd never known anyone who had gone away permanently before, and he didn't like the bruised feeling it gave him in the chest. It was a bad way to go too, and he worried that Grandma might have been frightened. It had been on the news, and the police had walked around her house in white jumpsuits, and Foster heard the word *misadventure* a lot. He supposed this meant Grandma had been planning an adventure and missed out on that on top of everything else, which made her dying even sadder, really. But then his dad had told him about the dragon fire, and it made him feel better.

Foster's mom had almost died, but that was a long time ago, and Foster knew about it mostly from the way she looked and the stories his dad told him. Foster's mom had an unusual face. Foster grew up with this face, so it never bothered him. It was the face that leaned over him at night to smell his breath in the random tooth-brushing check. It was the face that kissed his forehead after ministering to the slashed knee he got falling off his bike. It was the face that greeted him in the car after school. Foster knew her face was different from his—and his dad's—but it wasn't until he started school and saw the way other people looked at it that he began to feel self-conscious.

"Can you take me to school instead of Mom?" Foster asked his dad.

"Why?"

"Kids at school say Mom looks weird," Foster confessed quietly. "They make fun of her."

"Do they make fun of her, or do they make fun of you?" Dad asked.

"Umm . . ."

"Mom's got a different face because she had an accident."

"I know," Foster said. "Tell me the story again, Dad."

His dad put down the book they were sharing, took a breath that raised his shoulders high, and said, "Once upon a time, there was a princess imprisoned in a castle surrounded by a moat filled with giant sea snakes. She was the most beautiful lady in the kingdom. Knights came from far and wide and wrote songs about her and battled the snakes that prevented her escape. But she was waiting for her prince. She became so sad that she decided to call upon the old magic of her forefathers. This was a dangerous thing to do. Old magic was rarely used because when it gave you power, it took something in return. But she was lonely. A spell was given to her: the snakes would remain in the moat and she could walk from the confines of her prison across the drawbridge in safety."

"Oh, yes?" his mom said. Foster looked up to see her standing in the doorway, listening.

"Yes!" his dad continued. "But the moment she stepped onto the bank—the moment she gained her freedom— her face would forever bear the mark of the snakes she had charmed to win her escape. She walked slowly across the bridge and hesitated only a second before placing her toe on free ground. It was then she felt a great slithering inside her head, and all at once, one side of her face was paralyzed. She hid her face, sure that she would forever be completely alone."

Foster could almost feel the cold air shimmying off the dark water of the moat, clinging to his face.

"Then she heard a restless horse approaching, and she knew it was her prince. She stood before him, frightened and ashamed, but he saw in her crooked face a courage and strength that eclipsed any beauty he had ever seen. He knelt before her and offered her his fealty for the rest of her life."

"What's fealty?" Foster asked.

"Room and board in exchange for laundry and cooking skills," his mom said. Dad laughed.

"What happened to them after that?" Foster asked.

"They lived happily ever after," his dad said.

"Forever and ever?"

"Of course."

"Oh, for crying out loud," Mom said. But Foster saw she was smiling.

Foster heard other stories about his mom's face. He overheard conversations that had words and phrases in them he didn't understand, like *coma* and *traumatic injury*. He asked his mom what a coma was, and she said it was like being in a prison of sleep; so his dad's story satisfied him, and when asked at school about his mom, he repeated it to a wide-eyed audience.

"Your mom is not a princess," Blinky said. "You shouldn't tell lies."

"It's not a lie," Foster said. "It's a story."

"It's a stupid story!"

Foster wasn't worried when the stories first began to dwindle, because it happened in a creeping-up sort of way. Dad seemed too distracted to concentrate. The quiet at the dinner table became more and more frequent. Then his mom seemed to catch whatever bug it was that shushed his dad up. Foster knew that could happen. Whenever one of them got a cold, his mom would always say, "Now it'll go through all of us!" with a sort of good-humored resignation, and she was usually right. So when Mom too grew quiet (and a bit sad, Foster thought), he began to worry about this thing, whatever it was, going through him too. He began telling stories to himself and his toys—just a preventive thing, much like the vitamin C pills Mom gave him to prevent colds. They never worked.

Foster had faith in stories, though. Whatever changes were happening in his house and at the dinner table would surely, eventually, give way to another rollicking tale from his dad that would make his mom laugh again. So Foster became the dinnertime storyteller and carefully swallowed the gritty taste of not getting much response. Not much response at all.

Dad had a job that required a suit, and Foster liked suits. He'd decided that he would wear one when he grew up. It would be dark colored and have a crisp crease down the front of each leg. It would feel shiny to the touch and fit handsomely over a white shirt that smelled of ironing spray and Dad's cologne. At the kitchen table before work, Dad would tuck a napkin into his collar to make sure no runny egg or milk got on his tie. Foster liked the way the bright white shirt cuffs poked out and then retreated from the sleeves of Dad's jacket whenever he reached for the salt or a piece of toast. Sometimes Dad set his laptop up on the table next to his bowl or plate and scrolled through emails while he ate. He looked very important.

Sometimes he worked at night after he got home too. After baths and dinner, the laptop would appear again and Dad would *tap tap tap* away: tiny taps with the pads of his fingers. Not like the *click click* of Mom typing with fingernails that sounded like her high heels on a wood floor. Foster liked to sit at the table with Dad and work on a puzzle or read a book, occasionally glancing at Dad's merry fingers or hard-thinking face. Sometimes he would ask, "What are you doing now, Dad?" and Dad would say, "Making money for other people," without looking up.

Foster knew his dad was important without having to be told how or why. It wasn't just the suits or the making money for other people. It was the sense that his dad was relied on. Not just by him and Mom, but by lots of people. There were work phone calls at night and sometimes early in the morning, and Dad's voice was always different during these calls. It was slightly deeper; his words were fast and hooked together in such a way that they sounded like the car GPS when Mom accidentally set it to a foreign language. It was different from Dad's storytelling voice. This work voice had fewer colors and less movement. Foster found it a little bit scary. It was straight-edged, a voice that didn't waste time, a voice with no stories.

"Where does the suit voice come from, Dad?"

"The what?"

"That voice that's like a stranger's. The one you use on the phone."

"I have a stranger's voice on the phone? Is it this one? *More coffee, woman!*"

Foster jumped, but Mom laughed, standing at the kitchen sink, her back to them.

"I suppose you could call it part of my armor," his dad continued. "Like the suit. No knight sounds the same with his helmet on."

"Hot and echoey," Foster said.

"Very good!" Dad said.

When Dad's storytelling voice first started making an appearance during work calls, Foster thought it was funny. He thought Dad was doing it on purpose to make him laugh. First there would be a silence that seemed out of place. Foster knew when it was Dad's turn to talk because the tinny chirp of the person on the other end of the phone would stop. Where Dad would normally begin speaking immediately, or even get in early and cut the tinny chirp off, he started to fumble with his words. He seemed distracted, like he was searching for the next part of a story. It was as if he'd lost his train of thought, or, more likely, boarded another one.

Foster noticed that Mom saw it too. She didn't giggle about it like he did, though. She would stop what she was doing and look hard at Dad, as if her concentration alone could help Dad find the words he seemed to have lost. His face would look like he'd pulled a muscle. Sometimes he would take the phone away from his ear and just look at it before hanging up. But sometimes he would laugh and say something that didn't make sense in that high-pitched storytelling whisper of his.

Foster wondered if the person on the other end of the phone noticed the giggling or the silences. Mom was all concentration and no sympathy. It seemed somehow wrong to him in ways he couldn't possibly explain, even in a story. He kept waiting for Mom to find it funny too, and when she didn't, it made him nervous.

Foster's nervousness turned to hot and clammy the night Dad started to cry. Mom liked to read after dinner while Foster and Dad sat at the kitchen table and did their things. That was how Foster described it to her. On the way past, Mom ran her fingers across the top of Foster's hair as she retreated to the family room with a cup of tea and said, "What are you two up to?"

Foster solemnly replied, as he always did, "We're doing our things."

"And what things are they?"

"Secret things. Aren't they, Dad?"

"Oh, yes," Dad said without looking up as he shifted papers this way and that. "We're midritual here." Foster shuffled his books and drawings about, mirroring each of his dad's actions with the same attentiveness, brows drawn in, mouth puckered, and occasionally whistling on the hard exhale. It made him feel like he was helping.

When Dad's phone rang, he passed Foster a sheet of

paper covered in small indecipherable words and symbols and said, "Have a look over that for me, Fossie," before answering. Mom gave Dad a kiss on the top of the head and headed to the family room. Foster stared at the document in front of him and tapped a pencil thoughtfully.

Foster listened to Dad's armor voice for a while. It seemed in charge tonight. Foster began copying words from Dad's report onto his drawing paper, coloring in the holes in the letters. Foster was so absorbed in creating pockmarks in every word he copied that he didn't realize immediately that his dad had stopped talking. It was his pen not moving that alerted him. When he looked up, he saw Dad's face was red and wet, and Foster had to look hard to make himself believe his dad wasn't just sweating. But people don't sweat from their eyes. Foster let his fingers hover slightly above Dad's wrist before letting them land, because he was embarrassed for both of them. When his fingers finally touched down, Dad winced and recoiled his arm until it was curled up against his chest, his fingers in a knot under his chin. Foster slid quietly from his chair and went to the family room.

"Dad's crying," he said.

"Crying? I don't think so, Fossie." Mom didn't look up from her book.

"I think so," Foster said.

Mom looked at Foster then. She pressed her lips

together and stood. She left her book facedown on the couch, clearly expecting to be right back. Foster followed her into the kitchen, where she stood behind Dad's chair and leaned to the side to look at Dad's face. Her hands were resting on his shoulders. Foster stayed where he was, watching the back of them. Mom took the phone that was still pressed to Dad's ear from his hand, putting it to her own ear. She said, "Hello," and clearly someone answered because she listened then, making a few thoughtful noises like *mmm* and saying "I see" twice. Then, "He'll have to call you back," and the small *pip* of ending the call.

"Malcolm?" She said it cautiously, as if to a sleepwalker she didn't want to shock into wakefulness. When Dad's phone, still in Mom's hand, suddenly rang, all three of them yelped in such a way that Foster started to giggle. It was the yelp that was needed, the sudden blare of spiky noise into an increasingly uncomfortable silence. It snapped them all into a kind of action—small action, but Foster was grateful for it nonetheless. Mom took Dad's hand and led him down the hall toward their bedroom. She shut the door behind them, leaving Foster standing in the kitchen alone with a giggle still pressing on his lungs. He walked forward and closed Dad's laptop. Then he went to the couch and put Mom's bookmark inside her book, placing it on the coffee table.

Dad used the word *ritual* a lot. He said rituals helped make sense of the unfathomable, and that we didn't have enough of them. He said they didn't have to be fancy either. Even small rituals can coax people closer together, just like cinching the neck of a drawstring bag. Foster had a drawstring bag he kept library books in. He liked the sigh of the fabric sliding on the thin waxed rope that secured it. When it was shut tight, the neck formed a soft flower. Foster knew what his dad meant.

Foster's favorite day of the week was Sunday. Not just because it wasn't a school day, but because exactly the same thing happened on every Sunday. Other days, for all their sameness, came with all sorts of unpredictable stuff. Foster didn't mind surprises if they were good ones (he didn't like surprise spelling tests or trips to the dentist), but he liked his unsurprising routine more. The stuff Dad called ritual and looked forward to just as much as Foster did.

On Sundays Dad's phone stayed off and his laptop stayed shut. Sometimes they stayed in pajamas until eleven o'clock. Mom didn't rush to make the beds. Bathing was optional. Dad made pancakes with lemon and sugar, and Foster got to beat the batter.

"It doesn't have to be completely smooth," Dad said. "Some lumps are good."

"Okay," Foster said, allowing Dad to peek into the bowl.

"I said *some* lumps, Fossie. Keep going."

"Do you need help?" Mom asked, wandering into the kitchen with the newspaper under her arm.

"Honey, we're midritual here!" Dad said. He sounded all cross and put out, but Foster knew it was an act. Mom whacked Dad on the bottom with the rolled-up paper and strolled back toward the family room.

"What are we looking for, Fossie?"

"Ribbon consistency."

"Good man."

Sunday breakfast was always the same. It took a long time. They sat at the kitchen table and ate one pancake at a time. As soon as everyone had finished, Dad would get up and make three more so each serving was hot and crisp on the edges and warmed the cold lemon juice just enough to make some of the sugar crystals melt. Foster's fingers and lips would be glazed with the tart, sweet syrup until moments before they headed into town.

Going into town was one of Foster's favorite things to do with Dad. They played games in the car. I Spy, Who Can Spot Ten Red Cars First, and Foster's favorite: the Road Sign Game. Dad would call out a word from a sign, and Foster would have to use it in a sentence. Then they would switch. Sometimes Dad said that their alternate sentences had to string together to make a story. That was harder, but the story always teased itself out of randomness as if the road signs themselves were helping in the creation.

"Mirror!" Dad called out.

"Umm, there was this big mirror on the wall of the . . . castle and . . . people who looked in it saw . . ."

"Don't stop. This is good stuff. What did they see?"

"Magic things!"

"I love it! Pick the next word."

Foster studied the streetscape. Road signs, shop signs, signs on the sides of trucks. Some of the words he didn't know, but he didn't want to pick one that was too easy. Then he saw a shop he recognized. He knew what it was called because he'd been in there with Mom a lot.

"Tapestry!" Foster called out.

"Fantastic word!" Dad said, thumping the steering

wheel. "So. What the magic people saw when they looked in that mirror was a . . . tapestry of their possible futures."

"A picture made of lots of colored thread? And they can choose what they do next?"

"Yes! My turn to pick. Ah . . ."

"By following the color they like?"

"Yes! I choose—"

"But it's hard to follow colors in those big pictures that Mom does. They're all kind of together, Dad."

"It's magic, remember? I choose . . . *light!*"

Foster paused for some time. Dad didn't rush him. Dad always said there was no point in rushing good thinking. Then Foster said, "But if they couldn't choose, the mirror went dark and there was no light anymore."

"Good twist," Dad said. "Now people are looking at a dark pane of glass? Does it still reflect? What's your word, Fossie?"

"Why did you cry on the phone, Dad?"

"What?" Foster saw Dad's eyes flick momentarily to the rearview mirror. "I didn't cry on the phone, love."

"You did, Dad."

"No, I didn't, Fossie. Let me tell you something about mirrors. They have been used to tell the future for a long, long time. Anything that reflects has been used by magic people to predict the future—and sometimes change the future. There's a long storytelling tradition about prophets and seers looking into glass and seeing the future. So does your dark glass reflect? What's your word, Fossie?"

Foster watched all the words in the world whirl past him. The car seemed to be going too fast now for him to settle on a word. Foster felt a pain in his gut he didn't recognize. As Dad pulled the car into the parking lot, Foster felt his story word crawl from his clutched throat into his mouth.

"Dad? My word is *liar.*"

Foster's dad half turned in his seat. "Did you see that on a sign?" he asked.

Foster was sorry he'd said it right away. Dad didn't look confused or embarrassed at all. Foster couldn't bear the thought of Dad using the word in the next part of the story, so he unbuckled his seat belt and said, "Come on, Dad!"

Even though they were stuffed with pancakes, the first stop was always hot chocolate and shortbread. There were lots of choices of cookies and cakes, but Foster loved the way the sweet, buttery lozenge of shortbread dissolved away when he held it against the roof of his mouth. They would have races too—like who could dip the shortbread in their hot chocolate the longest and get it into their mouth before the piece broke off and had to be rescued with a spoon.

The coffee shop they went to was right next door to a

small secondhand bookshop. The lady who worked there knew them by name. Sometimes when they went in, she would have put books aside for Dad to look at. Dad always bought something. The shop smelled good too. "Smell of old stories," Dad said. The books Foster liked were on a bottom shelf at the back. His dad would sit on the floor with Foster, and they would flick through the books, sometimes stopping to read parts. Week to week the books would be the same, but Foster didn't care. He liked sitting on the floor with his dad, surrounded by the Sunday smells of brittle paper.

When they took their book haul home, Mom said, "Why do you go there? You don't know where any of those books have been."

"Tell her, Fossie."

"Because we don't know where they've been."

"Good man. Every one of these books has multiple stories to tell. Look at this one," Dad said, rummaging about in the bag. "The last reader put notes in the margin. Fascinating!"

"It's fascinating, Mom!" Foster said.

"Urghh. Go wash your hands, both of you," Mom said. But she was smiling, and she kissed Dad as he walked past.

Funny Forgetting

The story about his grandma's fire was the last story Foster remembered his dad telling him before he started to change. It stuck in Foster's mind as the last one, anyway. It was the last story Dad told without looking confused and getting mixed up in the telling. Sometimes he would start telling one story and then trail off on some unrelated happening from before Foster was born. It didn't happen all the time. Every now and then Foster would ask Dad to tell the grandma story again, almost like a test, and feel comforted if Dad could get through it.

"Dad, tell me about Grandma's dragon fire again," Foster said.

"Dragon fire," Dad said. "Did we read that one?" Foster would feel strangely embarrassed every time his dad lost a story. He didn't want to draw attention to the lost stories.

His dad began doing funny things when he first started

to forget, so no one was worried. Foster thought the funny things were funny too. Dad went out for dog food and came back with cat food, when the cat had been dead for five years. Once he forgot to take the plastic wrapper off the cheese slices before putting them into sandwiches, and then couldn't work out why he couldn't cut them in half. Foster and Dad giggled about it. But then the forgetting got less funny. Like when Dad got confused on the drive home from work and had to park on the side of the road to figure out where he was. The police found him parked there, looking muddled. They thought he was drunk at first. They put him in the back of the police car and called Foster's mom. Nobody laughed much about that.

The beginning of the forgetting was the worst, because Dad knew about it. He knew something was wrong. Once the forgetting really set in, it didn't seem to matter to him. But somewhere in between the funny forgetting and the not talking anymore, his dad had moments—just moments—of absolute clarity, which really hurt him. Foster could see that Dad knew. He knew there were things he used to know that were going away. Mom started to get angry at the silly things Dad sometimes did, and he'd go sort of pale, the color of a secondhand book page, and make little clicking noises in his throat to cover his confusion. Foster imagined the noises were Dad's memory trying to squeeze out, like air being pinched from the stretched neck of a balloon.

His dad started walking differently. The change in his walking paralleled his forgetting, as if he were trying to make himself smaller, less noticeable. He started shuffling like a tall person trying to conceal his height. He wasn't a particularly tall person, but he stooped anyway, dragging his feet so they scuffed the floor. You could hear him coming. It made Foster's mom mad. Sometimes Foster would stumble across Dad leaning against a doorframe or sitting in a corner—always still, always expressionless—and sometimes he wouldn't answer when Foster talked to him. It was scary to come across Dad without warning. The only way to be sure where Dad was at any time was if he was making his way from one part of the house to another. Then there was that rasping of his feet on the floor.

His dad would sit in the family room a lot fiddling with a tin that had belonged to Grandma. It was an old cookie tin that probably wasn't all that old, but it had a russet tarnish around the lid that made it look like a shoddy heirloom. Foster had gone through that tin himself once. It was full of musty-smelling bits and pieces that Grandma had obviously wanted to keep for some reason. A few photos, birth certificates, and letters, along with some other things that seemed insignificant: feathers, a couple of shells, old movie tickets. Somehow, though, Foster knew none of the things in that tin had been accidentally placed, and his dad picked through everything meticulously, regularly, as if they were triggers to his memory. Sometimes his dad would just hold the tin in his lap, running his fingers across the lid, and then raise and lower the lid—up, down, up, down—the hinges stiff and squeaky. Foster would watch him, and it was as if he were playing an instrument. He would carry that tin around with him, room to room, wherever he went.

The one place his dad never went anymore was the backyard. He used to love the backyard. They had one of the few big lots on the street. The distance from the back door to the back fence seemed miles and miles, and at the back fence, hunkered down like an arbor sentry, was a jacaranda. As soon as Foster could walk, his dad started taking him out into the backyard to catch balls and watch clouds and play fetch with Geraldine, their drooling mutt. Dad loved Geraldine. He said mutts were best. Purebreds were full of temperament and malaise. When Foster asked what that meant, Dad told him bad manners and bad health. Dad called Geraldine a genetic jigsaw of proper dogs. She had a crooked face and tender eyes. When the forgetting and shuffling got worse, Foster would hold Dad's hand and try to lead him into the backyard. But when Geraldine howled for a game of fetch now, it just seemed to upset Dad, and Mom told Foster to leave Dad be. That was when Foster would run out back and climb that jacaranda, just to get away for a little while, and sometimes he'd see his dad watching out the kitchen window, his stare rasping just like his walk.

Foster's feelings were tangling him up. No one was explaining to him how he should be feeling, and he didn't understand the feeling that was bothering him now. He'd see his dad standing in that crooked way of his at the kitchen window, and his pulse would clang like a screw in a tin can. When that first Sunday came and went without pancakes and shortbread, Mom didn't explain at all; she just poured Saturday cereal into a bowl for him and rubbed the top of his head. Foster suddenly recognized the thing that rolled over him and made him feel sick: Dad was going away somewhere all on his own. And Foster was already missing him.

D ad eventually had to drop back to part-time work. It was a type of stress leave, apparently. Foster asked Mom what Dad was stressed about, but she danced around the question in a way familiar to Foster—he was getting used to having questions answered in great detail that turned out to provide no answer at all. Dad could work from home now, Mom said. Work fewer hours, work in his pajamas if he wanted to. Mom said this last bit with a bright smile, as if it was meant to be a fine joke, but Foster found the idea of Dad not putting on a suit the last straw. It made him angry. Foster knew all about last straws. It was Mom's way of putting a full stop at the end of something, of declaring her refusal to entertain another moment of whatever it was that was creating the straws in the first place. So when Foster said with genuine indignation, "Well, that would be the last straw," expecting Mom to share in his anger, he was instead humiliated to find himself being laughed at.

Foster was pleased that at least Dad was still dressing for the doctor. They all went with him to the appointment, despite Dad's protests about being treated like a child. Foster wasn't allowed to go into the little room where the doctor did his examining. He had to wait in the ugly waiting room that always seemed to have one dead fish in the tank in the corner. He waited a long time—long enough for the room to get really full. He had to start breathing through his mouth because of the sweet-sweaty smell of too many sick bodies pressed together like paper dolls. He wished he had asked to wait in the car.

There was no talking in the car on the way home. Foster rolled his window down and filled his cheeks with fresh outside air until Mom snapped at him to put the window back up. "It's too cold," she said.

When they got home, Mom and Dad went into the kitchen to talk. It was quiet talk at first, but Foster had worked out that if he himself stayed really quiet, he became invisible. Either that or his parents thought he couldn't hear them. So he waited, and sure enough the volume began to rise. It seemed Dad had come back from the doctor with pills that frustrated him even more. Foster heard Dad say, "I'm not depressed!"

"You are, Malcolm. I can see it."

"If I'm depressed, it's because I can't work out why I'm having trouble concentrating. Why I can't remember things! I've worked with numbers all my life, and suddenly Excel looks like abstract art to me. That's justifiable, reasonable grounds for depression. There's no pill for a rational human response, is there! Why aren't they looking at what's *causing* this? Treating the symptom won't get me back to work, will it!"

It wasn't a question. Dad never asked questions when he was using his work voice, and he was using his work voice on Mom now.

"Just try them for a little while, *please*, Malcolm," Mom said. "The doctor said in a few weeks you'll feel better. So much better." It was a plea. Foster had a feeling Mom was pleading her own case, her own need to feel better, rather than Dad's. Mom didn't cope well with other people's illnesses. They made her fretful. When Foster was sick, he always felt a responsibility to get better as quickly as possible, and with the least amount of fuss and inconvenience. It wasn't that Mom didn't look after him, or was angry, but her hand on his brow always trembled and his vomiting made her gag. Dad had told Foster that perhaps her fear of illness came from having been so ill herself. It triggered something in her: a need to rush through and reestablish normal routine as quickly as possible. Illness set off a prickly alarm in her—a fear of frailty in people she loved.

"I'll consider it," Dad said.

"And perhaps some counseling. The doctor said—"

"I know what the doctor said!"

Dad never raised his voice, but he was raising it now. He slapped the air so hard with the words that Foster felt the sting himself. He wanted to step in. The need to say something was very strong, a burly knot deep in his heart. He tried to think of something he could say to fix this. Something that would stop the pleading and the raised voice. Maybe if he said something, it would remind them that he was in the room too.

But there was nothing to say. So Foster just walked over to his dad's side and took his hand. Dad looked down and smiled. Mom said, "Not now, Fossie."

The pills went into the bathroom cabinet. Mom told Dad to take one every morning after he had brushed his teeth. "You take it the same time every day," she said. "That way you'll remember. Please, Malcolm."

At first Dad took the pills. Foster would slide the mirrored door of the bathroom cabinet open and check the box. Each day a little blister on the sheet of pills would be popped, and the tiny cavity where the pill had sat would be empty. Foster would count them. But after a couple of weeks, the evidence of consumption became sporadic. Sometimes a pill would be gone. Sometimes it wouldn't. Foster was sure it didn't matter if Dad missed one occasionally, but when days began to pass with no indication of the packet having been disturbed, Foster became worried. He considered popping out the odd pill himself and hiding it, so Mom wouldn't get upset again. But just as he was formulating this plan, it became obvious that Mom was checking the box herself.

Mom began reminding Dad to brush his teeth. Sometimes Dad forgot to do that. It was like she was trying to prompt the pill taking through association, rather than just telling Dad to take it. She mustn't have liked his raised voice either. Then Foster noticed a Post-it appearing on the mirrored door of the cabinet. It always said the same thing: *Don't forget to take your pill.* It wasn't always the same note, though. Foster could tell because the color of the Post-it changed sometimes. But even with all this, Dad still didn't take his pill every day.

Then one morning when Foster sat at the kitchen table, he saw Dad's pill sitting on his plate next to a glass of orange juice. When Dad sat down, he asked, "What's this?"

"Your pill," Mom replied.

"I already took it."

"No, you didn't. I checked."

"I did. I took it."

"No. You didn't. And you haven't been taking it." Mom said this while leaning on the other end of the kitchen table. Foster didn't like the lean. He didn't like the

36

flattened palms or the arched shoulders or the unbrushed hair. It all made Mom look a bit wild, a bit ready for it. She was pouncy.

"Well, I'm not taking it again," Dad said.

"You haven't taken it!"

And then Dad yelled a word that Foster had heard before but knew that no one in his house ever, ever was allowed to say. He *yelled* it. Foster dropped his butter knife on his plate. It landed with a big clang. Mom and Dad both looked at him then, and he found himself in the middle of a moment as raw as a peeled scab. Dad didn't use bad words. He said the English language is full to capacity with descriptors for anything and everything, and that bad words are just lazy.

"You haven't taken it," Mom said in a quiet voice that Foster found more frightening than Dad's f-word. "I've been checking, Malcolm. You only have to do this one thing to make all this go away. And I can't help but think that your refusing to do so is a direct attack on me."

Dad looked hurt. It was a face Foster didn't see very much, and it made him feel sore. Dad stood so quickly that his chair scraped the floor. Then he strode out of the room.

Foster could hear him rummaging in the bathroom cabinet. Mom rolled her eyes at Foster, and he smiled a little bit because he was desperately in need of being aligned with one of them. He couldn't stand being out here on his own. When Dad returned to the kitchen, he was holding a box of pills. He flicked it across the table, like skipping a stone on a lake. It skidded to a stop right next to Mom's hand.

"Go on. Check again. Do it!" he demanded.

At first Foster didn't know if Mom was laughing or crying. She sat down, rested her head in her hands, and began shaking and making noises. When she looked up at Dad, Foster could see she was laughing, but laughing in such a way that there were tears coming out as well. Then she gave a big sigh and on the crooked edge of a declining snicker said, "Why are you doing this to me, Malcolm?"

Dad walked out of the room first. The bathroom door slammed. Mom followed. The bedroom door slammed. Foster leaned across and picked up the box of pills Dad had flung at Mom. It wasn't the box he'd been checking. He sounded out the name: *Tram-a-dol*. Under that was Mom's name on the label.

Bats in the Belfry

Mom had taken Dad back to the doctor with the notes she'd been keeping. Not just notes about Dad taking the wrong pills for weeks, but about all the other funny things he'd been doing as well. Foster had seen her writing in the notebook after dinner with her brow squeezed tight, and when he asked her what she was doing, she said she was keeping a diary about Dad. When Foster asked why, she said, "Because he will need to go for an assessment. Special tests."

"What for?" Foster asked.

"Just to find out if he's sick or not."

"He doesn't look sick," Foster said.

"Yes, I know."

"Does he feel sick, then?"

"Sometimes. In a way. When he's confused. When he forgets things. That doesn't feel good to him. Do you understand?"

Foster did understand, and he found it all mildly exciting. His dad had been to the doctor a lot lately, and having a sick dad had given him some authority among his friends at school. He was going through something, and he was listened to respectfully as he recounted exaggerations and outright fictions about his dad's mysterious sickness. It gave him some credibility to tell stories about his suffering. People were interested. And when someone would lean in and breathe "Is he going to die?" with all the respect owed someone about to lose a parent, Foster would drop his eyes and whisper, "We don't know yet." He never actually believed his dad was going to die, but it was thrilling to be the center of attention when he'd previously had hardly any attention at all.

It was at school that he got his first inkling that something quite serious might be going on.

A week after the special tests, Mom and Dad went back to the doctor to get the results. At first Foster was relieved when his mom spat out the diagnosis across dinner. She didn't mean to spit it. She hadn't meant it to sound angry and mean. But her face collapsed around the syllables as they skimmed her lips. The last syllable, the "ease," was barely audible. The relief Foster felt was in the word *disease*. Diseases have cures. He said, "Oh!" rather hopefully, and Dad patted him on the back. Apparently Dad wasn't depressed at all. Just like he'd said all along.

The next day Foster went to school with his new knowledge, ready to impart the next installment to friends whose lives were nowhere near as interesting as his. He told the small knot of boys gathered around him, "My dad has Alzheimer's disease."

There was a pause. A couple of them looked confused. Then James Maher, whom everyone called Jimmy, snorted and said, "Old-timer's disease, you mean."

Some of the others started to laugh. Then Foster was confused. His only knowledge of old people came from his grandma. Old people had skin like crepe paper and smelled of cough syrup and mothballs.

"My dad's not old," Foster said. "This is serious." His *"this is serious"* was far from compelling. It was a quasi-question.

"This is what it is, Fossie," Jimmy continued. "Your old man will go crazy and die. Well, he'll go crazy and then die. But he'll be crazy for a long time first."

"My dad's not old!" Foster repeated, a bit louder than he meant to. He was horrified. He was still standing there, twitchy and indignant, as most of them wandered away. Someone leaned in and breathed, "Is he going to go crazy and die?"

Foster dropped his eyes and whispered, "We don't know yet."

For the rest of that school day, Foster couldn't

concentrate. Jimmy Maher's words formed a ropy nimbus in the center of his brain that no amount of teacher admonishment could dispel. He couldn't add numbers together, as they seemed to grow legs on his page and march away before they could be calculated. He couldn't write a story, because no ideas would penetrate the smog of panic that had settled in the back of his throat. He couldn't color a picture, because his fingertips were as flailing and obstinate as fat, bald babies. Stupid Jimmy. Putting crazy in his head like this. Stupid Jimmy. Stupid Dad. Foster had a hole in his heart the size of the moon.

It never occurred to Foster to question Jimmy's assessment of the diagnosis that had landed on the kitchen table the evening before in a volley of Mom's spittle. Foster floundered between the two reference points he had been given since his dad had patted him on the back for his optimism. Alzheimer's and crazy.

When Mom picked Foster up after school, he wanted to ask her if the crazy was real. But he didn't. Mom had a certain expression that closed her face like a door. It was her don't-talk-to-me face, and she was wearing it the entire journey home. When they did get home, it was to smells and sounds Foster liked. His mom had been cooking. There was the metallic odor of Brussels sprouts and the sweet whiff of a roasted meat crust. Foster liked sprouts. Slathered in butter and salt, cooked hard so they popped in his mouth. The fire was alight. It cracked and spat as it consumed the damp bits and wood sap. The TV was on. There was a time when Dad wouldn't have been home from work yet, but today he was sitting in front of it. Foster walked up to the side of the recliner his dad sat in and leaned on the arm. His dad turned slightly and then turned back to the program he was watching. It was a little kid's show. Foster didn't even watch it anymore. Some presenters in bright outfits were singing about brushing your teeth.

"Dad?"

No response.

"Dad!"

"Yes, Fossie?" his dad answered without taking his eyes from the TV.

"Dad, are you going crazy?"

Dad smiled, and Foster didn't know if he was smiling at him, his question, or the TV. That same smile appeared a lot lately. He had seen Mom on the receiving end of that smile and had seen her look sad about it. He had heard Mom describing that look to someone on the phone as being the memory of response, or how to respond, to a gentle tone of voice.

"What?" Dad said.

"Are you going crazy?" Foster asked again.

"Foster!" Mom was behind him, standing in a bent

way with a wild face. She looked like an overwrought pipe cleaner. "Leave your dad alone. Go find something to do until dinner."

Foster snapped upright at his mom's admonition. Then he ran outside and climbed the jacaranda, simmering in branches that held him like a dancer's arms.

Eggs
and
Emancipation

Foster had a set of plastic army men that he would stage battles with. Dad had taught him about some famous battles, and they used to re-create the best battles among the blankets and pillows on Foster's bed. Foster liked the battles for people better than the battles for land. He found it easier to fight for a few inches of quilt if there was a rescue involved. So he would put some men on Pillow Top Mountain under an overturned clothespin basket and fight for their release. He would make all the noises too—the prisoners wailing and the army chanting and weapons popping and grinding toward victory.

Dad had told him that history was important. So one day Foster put only one plastic soldier under the clothespin basket. It was his favorite—a general—someone who usually directed the fight rather than participated in it. Someone who decided history rather than died for it. He stood the general up, proud and defiant in the center of a moat of socks, and called the general Dad.

Foster stormed the clothespin basket regularly. Again and again his army overpowered the bulwark of the enemy, dragging the general back down the hill to safety. The troops would celebrate by reminding the general of other great victories. They would talk about where they'd been and what they'd done before, and the general would guffaw and snort and say, "I don't remember that!" The general's history only existed now in the memories of his troops. Foster wondered whether something forgotten stopped existing altogether. He decided it might be a good idea to write the general's stories down so that they'd be real history, just like the stories in the books on Dad's bookshelves.

Foster would put his dad back under the clothespin basket and spend the entire next day at school thinking about future rescue approaches. His thinking about it set a drowsy hum louder than a chainsaw in his quietest insides. It was comforting because it drowned out other thoughts.

There was still interest in Foster's sick dad among his small cluster of friends, but the interest was different now. Foster couldn't quite decipher the change, but he knew instinctively that it had to do with Jimmy Maher broadcasting his interpretation of the general's illness to some of the older boys. He heard it said that his dad had had a breakdown, which he thought was silly because Mom didn't even let him drive anymore. Foster heard her telling the neighbor, Miss Watson, that she didn't mind him getting lost, but what if he forgot what a traffic signal meant and killed someone? Miss Watson had smiled and said, "Better keep your wits about you, then." Foster wasn't sure what wits were, but he made a decision to find his and make sure he held on to them too. Other boys at school called the general mental, and Foster would feel a sharp pain in his gut.

"He's not mental," Foster said, all the while worrying that if it had been so easy for the general to have his wits break off and fall down, then what was to protect him and his mom from the same fate? Since Mom had gotten her second job, she had twice forgotten to make Foster's school lunch. She had shoved lunch money at him at the last minute as if that had been her intention all along, but Foster saw a hole in her head that she had probably caught from his dad.

Mom had taken a second job at night packing meat onto trays for shops soon after the general stopped going to work—when he started watching TV a lot and wandering around with Grandma's tin. Mom had explained to Foster that his dad was beginning to forget things and would forget more things as time went along. They had to help Dad and be kind and happy and not bother him too much with things that didn't matter. She had not been specific about what mattered and what didn't. Foster had not been worried then. He could be kind and happy and not bothersome. He became very bothered, though, when it became increasingly apparent that his mom was not being kind and happy herself. She worked during the day and at night, and when she was home, she seemed sad and jittery. She said "Please, Fossie, I'm tired" a lot, and talked on the phone to new and strange people more than she talked to him.

Foster decided to confront his mom. It wasn't enough to be told to leave his dad alone and go and find something else to do when at any moment Foster might smell his own flesh burning and forget he was supposed to beat himself out. He started with, "Can we get Dad back?"

They were in the car on the way home from school. His mom waited until they were at a stoplight before saying, "What do you mean, Foster?"

"Get him back. Can we get him back from wherever he's going?"

"Your dad isn't going anywhere."

Foster wondered if that was a lie meant to comfort him or whether his mom really didn't see the same retreat in the general's eyes that he did. He tried again. "Will he ever get back what's going away?"

"Things will come and go," Mom said after a short pause. "I don't want you to worry about it."

"What things that have gone will come back? And when they come back, will they stay and new things go, or can the things that have gone once go again?"

"Oh please, Fossie, I'm tired."

They drove on in silence, stopping at the shops. Foster stayed in the car while Mom went in for eggs. Foster was tired of eggs for dinner. They didn't have a lot of his favorite foods anymore because Mom had to get a nap in before she went to her night job. They had a lot of eggs, beans on toast, and things that could be heated up in the microwave. As they pulled away from the shops, Foster said, "Some kids at school say Dad's mental."

"Why on earth would they say that?"

"Because his brain's got a disease."

"Just ignore them."

They pulled into the driveway in silence, a little crease on Foster's forehead. As he slipped out from the front passenger seat, one foot caught on the shoulder strap of his backpack. Recognizing the arcing of the ground toward him, he threw his hands wide to catch the car door frame and save himself. The eggs slid from his lap and landed, carton top down, on the driveway. He was squatting beside the carton, turning it over and cautiously lifting the lid, when his mom walked around to his side of the car.

The translucent, mucousy smear of broken eggs spattered the carton and the concrete, one perfect globe of yolk quivering among shards of shell. Foster said, "Look, Mom! They're not all broken!"

When he looked up, his mom was leaning against the car door crying. Foster found her crinkled face in that moment as horrifying as a sea snake.

Foster had an aunt who didn't visit much until his dad started bringing strange things home from the super-market. Somehow that piqued her interest. When she talked to his mom about it, Foster felt funny. He couldn't quite work out why. It wasn't the words she used. She said nice things, helpful things. She suggested putting sticky notes up on the doors of different rooms of the house so that Dad would recognize where he was and maybe remember why he went in there. She suggested doing the same to label cupboards and drawers so Dad would know their contents. She'd bought a book, you see. Foster's mom smiled as she listened and said she really didn't think those things were necessary yet. She tried to explain that she was in touch with the Association and they, along with the Doctor, were monitoring things and offering help and support, but it was very good of Aunty to offer to help too. But Foster felt something wasn't right. There was a tension in Mom's voice and Aunty seemed to be enjoying herself too much.

Foster was very glad the Association and the Doctor were involved. His dad had told him stories about the Association of Knights Templar. They were an ancient and secret organization that went on long journeys to find lost things. When they found the lost thing they were looking for, they would take it back to an enchanted underground keep, where they would guard it forever. No one knew where the special place of guarded lost things was, but there were stories about what was hidden and protected there. King Arthur's Round Table, Pandora's box, the crown jewels of King John "the Bad," and the treasures of Montezuma, to name just a few. Foster had listened with his heart pounding. He pictured a dark cavern that eternally glistened with the refracted light of burning torches warming the patina of precious metals and jewels. Foster knew that if anyone could find his dad's memory, it would be the Association. They were looking for it now. He just knew it. Foster wasn't sure how Doctor Who could help, but it couldn't hurt to have him on board.

The first time Dad went missing, Aunty was around with her book almost immediately. Foster had noticed that Mom and Dad went out in the car together and that only Mom returned. He wasn't worried at first. Dad had lots of appointments lately, and perhaps this was a longer one and Mom had decided to come home and go back to collect Dad later. Foster still wasn't concerned when he saw Mom running from the car to the front door. Or even when she dropped her handbag on the floor by the front door and started running from room to room calling Dad's name. But when she grabbed Foster by the shoulders and knelt down so her good eye was level with his and said, "Have you seen your dad?" in a squeaky way, Foster felt frightened. Miss Watson from next door carefully placed the book she had been reading down on the couch beside her. She always brought a book along when she watched Foster, and she never read the story out loud to him. She was not his favorite babysitter.

That was when Aunty pulled into the driveway. She got out of her car so fast that she left the car door open and dropped her book. Soon there was a huddle of them—Mom, Aunty, and Miss Watson—standing in the kitchen. Mom and Aunty started making phone calls. They talked loudly to different people over the top of each other, so Foster found it difficult to understand what was going on at first. But the air tasted different, and as the panic among the grown-ups grew, Foster felt it settle on him like a tetchy heat. His dad was missing. His dad was lost. Mom had lost Dad. That was when it burst out of him: the most sensible thing, the most obvious thing, "Call the Association!"

All three women stopped and looked at Foster as if they had forgotten he was even in the room. Then Mom said, "Yes, Fossie—good idea," as she scrolled through the saved numbers in her phone.

The next few hours were so fraught that Foster found himself laughing nervously at the stress around him. He didn't know why. It was the only thing he could do to cope with the lack of control exhibited by the people who were supposed to be in control of everything all the time. It seemed that after Dad's appointment, Mom had stopped at the supermarket to buy eggs. She explained to Dad that she would be back in a few minutes and left him in the car. Mom was back in a few minutes, but Dad was gone. At first she didn't panic, thinking he had just followed her into the shop. A cursory, followed by thorough, search of the aisles revealed nothing. Mom had then enlisted the aid of a shop assistant, who had found it incomprehensible that Mom was so upset about a grown man going for a walk. The man checked out the back of the shop where only employees could go, but Dad wasn't there either. That was when Mom started driving the streets in widening circles. She also called Aunty. It was Aunty who suggested Dad might have made his way home.

Calling the Association didn't seem to have the immediate calming effect Foster believed it would. Mom seemed annoyed with them on the phone. She said things like "Yes, yes, we've already done that!" and "Can't you do something?" and then hung up looking teary and wild. That was when she and Aunty decided to go back out in their cars and look around. They planned it first: who would go where. It was a reconnaissance akin to the greatest battles on Pillow Top Mountain, and Foster was reassured.

Foster waited, sitting on the back of the couch looking out the front window. Miss Watson read her book and occasionally exhaled loudly from her nostrils. Foster didn't think anything of it when the taxi pulled up in front of the house. He was curious, that's all, because he'd never been in a taxi. He watched the taxi driver get out and go around to the passenger side. He then took the passenger gently by the elbow and eased him up and out of the front seat. It was Dad, and he was annoyed. Foster could see that. He yanked his arm away from the taxi driver and staggered back. Then he sat down on the curb and started yelling stuff. Foster didn't even notice Miss Watson come up behind him until he felt her loud nostrils on his ear. She walked to the front door as the taxi driver began walking up the front path.

Foster ran by them both. Miss Watson's "Get back inside!" broadsided him, but he kept going. Foster reached his dad and squatted down next to him. Dad was covered in grass and sand. It was sticking to his clothes and all through his hair, and there were dry leaves protruding from the collar of his shirt. He had a smudge of dirt on his face, and the bottoms of his trousers were wet. Foster touched his dad on the top of his head and said, "Come on, Dad."

Foster heard the taxi driver saying, "I'll need to be paid," as he led his dad back up the path to the front door. Miss Watson fumbled in her purse and Foster heard her say, "You had no right to take a fare without permission! Can't you see he's not right in the head?" Once inside, Foster led his dad to his favorite chair in front of the TV. That was when his dad looked straight at him and said, "Hiya, Fossie!"

Foster couldn't think of anything to do to express his relief other than start picking the debris out of his dad's hair. That was when he noticed Miss Watson. She looked as if she'd been slapped upside the head with a wet fish. Foster knew that was what she looked like because Dad had said that exact same thing about people who had the same expression on their faces as Miss Watson did now. But then her face changed in a way Foster didn't like.

She started quietly, "Where do you think you've been? Do you have any idea how much trouble you've caused? Everyone's out looking for you. Even the police are out looking for you!" Then her voice got louder. "A whole day wasted because you can't do as you're told and sit still in a car for five minutes! Well? What do you have to say for yourself? You wander in here as if nothing's wrong? She ought to tie you to a chair. She ought to put you away!"

Foster watched Miss Watson's face, so screwed up and hot-looking, in disbelief. Then he watched his dad's face sink like a pothole under the weight of the scolding. Miss Watson tramped to the phone then and called Foster's mom. Her voice was calm and sweet on the phone to Mom, all relief and comfort. She said "I've found him" as if the weight of her concern alone had drawn him up the front path like a giant fishing lure. She said "Don't worry" and "He's fine" and "You're welcome," and after she'd hung up, she returned to the family room, sat opposite Foster's dad, and hissed, "Now I get to sit here until she gets home because you can't be left alone with your own child. And I'm not going anywhere until I am fully reimbursed for that taxi. Foster, go wait in your room."

Foster didn't move.

"I said, go wait in your room!"

Foster hooked his fingers around his dad's hand and then gently, tentatively, shook his head very slowly. That one tiny headshake, that one small act of defiance, took so much of Foster's courage that it exhausted him. He stayed by the general's side until his mom arrived home.

Missing Mussels

Mom and Aunty were very grateful to Miss Watson. Mom was crying as she hugged her. Aunty flicked through her book and said it was obviously time for a name tag, which made Foster think of school trips he had been on when the teacher would slap a sticker on his sweater with "Foster Sumner" written on it under the name of his school. His dad would look like he had just gotten off a school bus if he had a big yellow sticker on his sweater. They couldn't do that to him. Maybe they could make him look like one of the teachers or something.

"Maybe we could make him look like a teacher or something," Foster said. No one seemed to be listening to him. Miss Watson was making huffing noises about forking out for the taxi fare.

"Yes, yes, of course," Mom said, retrieving her purse. She didn't have enough cash on her, though. She handed over what she had and said, "I'll have to owe you the rest, Miss Watson. I'm so sorry."

"Well, I'll need it back as soon as possible."

"Of course you will, and I'll bring it to you as soon as I can. It's just that I only have enough money to pay you for the babysitting right now. I'm terribly sorry."

"And I'm afraid that will be more too, of course. I did stay longer today due to your . . . situation."

Everyone looked a bit stiff-necked then. Foster felt like Miss Watson expected Mom to say more, and Mom did not know what more to say. He noticed the good side of Mom's mouth was beginning to droop, which happened sometimes when she was very upset or very tired. It made Foster feel sour in his gut. Miss Watson broke the silence with, "I *am* on a pension, Mrs. Sumner."

That was when Aunty, leading Miss Watson to the front door, said, "Yes, well, thanks very much, Myra. I'd finish you off myself but I don't have any cash on me either. We'll make sure you get exactly what's coming to you."

"Wait. The taxi," Mom said. "I need to get in touch and thank the taxi driver."

Miss Watson turned and said, "I already did that, Mrs. Sumner."

"But I need to know what happened. Where he was," Mom persisted.

"I don't remember the name of the taxi company, Mrs. Sumner."

"You didn't get a receipt?" Aunty asked.

"No," Miss Watson said.

There was another one of those silences that made Foster look up from grooming his dad. Then he said, "It looked like a police car, Mom. It had stripes down the side and big numbers on the doors."

"I know who that is," Aunty said. She took Miss Watson's elbow then, the same way the taxi driver had taken Dad's, and opened the front door. Miss Watson pulled herself from Aunty's fingers and looked directly at Foster.

"You be a good boy," she said. Then she left.

"What a horrible woman," Aunty said, pushing the door shut. Then, "I'll put the kettle on. Want to help me, Fossie?"

Foster watched Aunty moving about the kitchen in a snappy, efficient way, popping tea bags in mugs, filling the kettle, shaking the milk. Foster thought about all the other times the kettle had been put on to celebrate something or get serious about something. It was the first thing grown-ups did. It was the herald of the post-battle analysis, be it good or bad. "I'll put the kettle on" meant something was going to be talked about. He heard the TV being switched on in the family room; then Mom walked in and sat down at the kitchen table.

"I have to be at work soon," she said.

"Took a Saturday shift?" asked Aunty.

"Yes. I thought . . . but now I'm not sure . . ." Mom glanced back toward the family room.

"Well, you've got time for a cup of tea. I'll make it. You go call the taxi company." Aunty handed Mom a piece of paper. "Pretty sure this is the company. If not, just call them all. Whoever it was will sure as hell remember this fare!"

Someone did remember the fare. Mom told them all about it. Dad had ended up so far from the supermarket he walked away from that she couldn't work out how he got there. He must have taken the footbridge that crossed the highway, and he must have moved fast. It never occurred to Mom, or Aunty, that he would take that footbridge. It should have. He was walking home. Not to his home now, but to the house he grew up in.

"Oh my God," Aunty said.

Dad had told Foster stories about the little house he grew up in. It was always full of people. His brothers and sister were older than him, so their friends were always around. He said it was one of the last houses he knew of that had a combustion oven, so it was hot inside during summer. It was on those broiling summer days that he and his elder brothers would walk the long way from their house to the river. There was no highway then, and no footbridge. When they got there, they would swim and pick fat bearded mussels off the rocks, which they took home in buckets of briny water. Grandma would throw them in a big pot with just a smidgen of that brackish river swill, and they would sit in the backyard and suck them out of their shells with nothing but a little salt and lemon juice.

"Sometimes," Dad had said, "you'd get some of that silky tuft from the shell stuck between your teeth, but we didn't care. They were so sweet. Better than lollipops!"

Dad had been wandering down the street only a couple of blocks from his old house when the taxi driver saw him. He had stopped and asked if Dad was all right. "I thought he'd been the victim of a crime," he told Mom. So the driver had put him into the taxi and was going to take him to a police station when Dad gave his address. It wasn't until they were well on their way home that Dad became angry with the taxi driver for taking him so far out of his way. No amount of explaining on the part of the taxi driver could calm Dad. The taxi driver told Mom he hoped he had done the right thing. Mom told him she was very grateful.

"He was going home for mussels," Foster said. Aunty smiled.

"Well, I haven't spent nearly enough time with my brother lately, so I think I'll stay for a visit while you're at work if that's okay," she said. Then, getting up so fast her chair scraped across the floor and almost toppled backward, she said, "Shoot, I didn't lock the front door when—"

"I did," Mom said. "And thank you."

That night Foster and his dad helped Aunty make dinner. They sat around the kitchen table and grated carrots and opened cans of tomatoes, and Aunty made a big pot of meat sauce that filled the house with the fragrance of home. And for the first time in a long time, Dad told a story. He told the story of the river and its lavish harvest of mussels in shells as black and shiny as ebony armor. They colonized the crags formed by dragon talons and birthed the pearls that adorned the sea princess's crown.

Bottoms in the Big Shops

Dad missing, even for such a short period of time, suddenly made those funny things he'd been doing lately less funny. Things like putting his clothes on inside out. Or storing fruit in the oven. Things they would usually tease him about, things they all giggled about and tried not to take too seriously, suddenly became suspicious signposts on the road toward Dad possibly making a break for it again. Mom wouldn't leave Dad at home alone with Foster when she had to go out, so Foster was roped in on drives to the shops, drives to the pharmacy, drives to the library. Anytime Mom faced the possibility of having to get out of the car and leave Dad for even a minute, Foster became the wingman, the babysitter. He resented it. Dad seemed blissfully unaware of any change in the behavior of those around him, and Foster resented that too. Mom said that trying to get Dad in and out of the car—and trying to get him to follow her around—was excruciating. She actually used that word on the telephone to someone. She said it was worse than dealing with a toddler.

Foster had gotten lost once when he was little. He hadn't realized he was lost at first. They were all at the Big Shops, as Mom called them—a complex as vast as a town, where you wouldn't see the sky for hours. For all the space inside, Foster always felt like he was being squeezed out of it by limbs and music and walloping voices, all competing for air and legroom. Foster used to like the Big Shops, before he became old enough to have to wait in the car with Dad. He liked all the voices and the rushing around. It was what he imagined the inside of a beehive would be like.

Foster remembered not being terribly concerned when he did realize he was lost. In fact, he hadn't even registered it in that way. He had felt utterly blameless. After all, his mom had lost *him*. It had taken only a moment. He had turned away from them to follow the foghorn bellow of a child being denied something she wanted, and when he turned back, the bottom immediately in front of him was neither Mom's nor Dad's. He instinctively had taken a step backward, having an inkling this sort of closeness to strangers was not okay, and then watched as the strange bottoms walked away, leaving a hole in the crowd empty of any clothing he recognized. He had spun around a few times, and then, completely confident that his parents would find him and find him quickly, taken the opportunity to wander.

He hadn't noticed the time passing at first. There were lots of things to see. When a lady had leaned down next to him and asked, "Are you lost?" he had told her "No" without hesitation. His first feelings of concern had coincided with feeling hungry. It had been a long time since breakfast and they were going to have lunch at the Big Shops. It was then he had decided to change his approach to the situation, and rather than just looking at all the things there were to see, he would also start looking for his parents. Anger hadn't taken too long to settle in after that. They had lost him and clearly weren't looking very hard for him. Maybe they had decided to have lunch before searching. Maybe they hadn't even realized they had lost him. Maybe he had turned invisible.

His strolling had given way to trotting, then running. He had started pushing on people to get them out of his way. He had wanted to go back to the place the strange bottoms first appeared, but he had wandered far enough away to not even be sure of the direction. He had pressed his back up against a shop window, just outside the pounding drive of the foot traffic, when he had finally seen Mom striding toward him, using her hands to part knots of shoppers, his dad only steps behind her.

It was the relief he felt at seeing them that allowed him to recognize how frightened he had been. His palms had been slick on the window glass. He had been smiling when Mom finally reached him. Still smiling when she had gripped him by the upper arm, hoisted him to his tippy-toes, and slapped him hard across the backs of his thighs.

Foster remembered the humiliation to this day. The rest was just a blur. His dad quickly stepping in, his mom's tears, her apology, the looks on people's faces. Being pulled through the crowd like a naughty boy. Because his mom had lost him.

And now that Mom had also lost Dad, Foster was being treated like a naughty boy again. *Get in the car, sit in the car, wait here, don't argue, I won't be long, I'll be right back.* It wasn't fair. She said he was too young to leave at home alone, but Foster suspected Dad was too crazy to leave alone in the car. He was even being treated like a naughty boy by Miss Watson from next door. And all because this was all so "excruciating," whatever that meant.

Foster began to hope his dad would try another escape. He was even tempted to provoke it and go with him. Dad had proven he was capable of finding his way home. So maybe this time they could stay away just a bit longer, long enough perhaps for Mom to be searching in the dark. They could watch for headlights coming their way and then dive into shrubs to avoid detection. That would be a real adventure. Foster wouldn't be invisible anymore, not after a thing like that.

"Wait here. I'll be right back," Mom said, cracking the car windows a bit and locking them in.

Dad immediately started trying the back doors. *Rattle-thump. Rattle-thump.* Foster knew where the child lock was. He knew how to unlock it. He imagined Mom coming out of the pharmacy and finding the car empty, just like she deserved. The thought pleased him.

Instead he got onto his knees and swung around to face his dad, who was still wrestling with the back door handles. He said, "It's all right, Dad. Want to play a game with me?"

"Hiya, Fossie!"

"I spy with my little eye, something beginning with . . ."

Christmas
Socks and
Cornflakes

Aunty always believed that Dad had married down. Foster didn't know what that meant, but he had heard it said. He heard Aunty say it to someone he didn't know at a Christmas lunch once, and he heard Mom repeat it to Dad in an angry way. Foster always imagined "down" to be a place, a destination, so he assumed Dad had gone down somewhere to marry Mom, down to a place Aunty clearly didn't like. But Dad had married Mom in a church. Foster had seen the pictures. And everyone liked church. Except Aunty, apparently.

They didn't go to church very often. Mainly Christmas and Easter, or if a baby was born and had to be blessed. That's why they went to church on the day Dad wet his pants. Someone Foster didn't know had had a baby, and in Foster's family, they got babies blessed lickety-split. At least that's what Dad used to say. "Get that kid in a font fast! Lickety-split!" Mom would laugh. When Foster had asked what the hurry was, Dad said the family threw so many bad seeds that they had to get the finger of God on board as soon as possible. Mom said, "Malcolm!" in a shocked way, but she was still laughing. Foster didn't understand the whole gardening reference, but he laughed too. And Dad winked at him.

Getting ready to go out took longer than it used to, and Foster was relied on to get ready without much help because Mom had to help Dad. Foster didn't mind. He liked getting ready to go out somewhere special. There was a tasty anticipation in it. They hadn't been out all together for a while now, unless it involved Dad and Foster staying in the car, so Foster was excited. Mom didn't seem excited.

Their bedroom door was shut, but Foster could hear them. Dad had been looking forward to getting the finger of God on the baby for weeks now. Every time Mom reminded him of the upcoming event, Dad would hear it as if for the first time and be very pleased. He would ask whose baby it was over and over and Mom would tell him again and again, each time with the same enthusiasm. But now it sounded as if Dad didn't want to get dressed. Foster could hear Mom pleading with Dad, a brittle edge of frustration sharpening her tone every now and then. Foster had been ready for a while, sitting at the kitchen table making little creases in the skin of an apple with his thumbnail. Mom walked in looking pretty. Foster thought she always looked pretty, but on occasions when photographs might be taken she arranged her hair on one side like a curtain of ribbons to gently rest against her bad eye. She smelled of hairspray and Red Door. That was her perfume. Sometimes, just lately, Foster would quickly squirt himself with it before he left for school so he could smell Mom all day.

"You look lovely, Foster," she said. "Very handsome." Then she pulled her phone from her handbag and left a message for Aunty. She said they might be late.

Foster's thumbnail had just penetrated the apple skin, something he avoided at all costs because he didn't like the sensation and it made Mom angry, when Dad appeared in the doorway. Mom's back was to him so Foster saw him first. Foster started to giggle.

Dad was wearing a pair of novelty Christmas socks he'd been given two years ago by Santa. He only wore them at Christmas. They had all sorts of shiny bits on them, some of which hadn't fared too well in the washing machine. They weren't pulled up properly either and gathered in loose folds around his ankles. Other than that he was completely naked.

"Mom," Foster said, "Dad's got his Christmas socks on."

Mom turned around and immediately dropped her

phone into the bowl of cornflakes that had been sitting on the kitchen table since yesterday morning. Mom didn't clean up as much as she used to. The milk had mostly been absorbed, leaving a kind of papier-mâché mulch in the bottom of the bowl. Foster watched Mom's phone sink a little before leaning forward and peeling it out of the curdy cereal.

"Malcolm!"

"My clothes were itching me," Dad said, just as Mom's phone began to ring. It didn't sound right.

Foster picked some wet cornflakes off the screen and answered. "Hello?"

Mom stepped across to Dad and gently took his elbow with one hand, awkwardly screening him with the only thing readily within reach: a tea towel.

"Malcolm, where are your clothes? We have to leave soon."

"Mom, it's Aunty. She wants to know how long we'll be."

"Where are we going?" Dad asked.

"To church, Malcolm. The baptism." Mom began easing Dad out of the kitchen and back toward the bedroom.

"Dad has taken all his clothes off," Foster said into the phone.

"Who's getting baptized?" Dad asked.

"Well, he's got his Christmas socks on," Foster said.

"Pippa had a baby," Mom said. "So you must get dressed."

"My clothes were itching me."

"Then we'll find you something else to wear. You've been looking forward to this, Malcolm."

"Aunty's coming over!" Foster called as Mom rushed down the hall with Dad.

"Oh, just tell her we're not going!" Mom called back.

"We're not going," Foster said. Then, "Sorry, Mom, she's already hung up!"

"We have to go!" Dad said. "Better get that kid in the font lickety-split!"

"Call her back, Fossie! Tell her we're not going!"

Foster scrolled through the contact screen on the phone. He blew into the little hole on the bottom of the phone where the charger cord went and it exhaled a tiny mist of moisture. Then he shook the phone and touched the screen to call Aunty.

"Aunty? Mom says we're not going. Can I come with you?"

Aunty didn't say much. When Foster hung up, he called out, "Mom? Aunty said a bad word!"

Pee and Prayer

Everyone was quiet in the car on the way to the church. It was the sort of quiet that felt like it should be filled. Aunty drove and Mom and Dad sat in the backseat. Foster got to sit in the front a lot lately. Sitting in the front used to feel like a treat; now it felt more like a penalty. The backseat used to come with conversation and games. The front seat came with instructions like "Get in" and "Seat belt."

When Dad started humming a tune into the tight quiet, Foster considered joining in until Mom patted Dad's wrist and gently shushed him. That was another word Foster had heard a lot lately. *Shush.* They used to sing and tell stories in the car, but lately Mom's tolerance for voices dropped off the moment they left the house. Foster thought it was unfair to make everyone shush just because Mom was embarrassed to be out with them. She seemed to feel voices in her skin. They made her fidget.

There was a lot of shushing and shuddering, which made Foster want to deliberately read road signs out loud. When they rounded the final corner and saw the church up ahead, Aunty began to chuckle quietly under her breath.

"What?" was all Mom said.

"He's still got his Christmas socks on," Aunty said.

"Don't talk about him as if he's not here," Mom replied.

"Hey, Malcolm!" Aunty adjusted the rearview mirror and tapped it with one finger. "Malcolm! I said you've still got your Christmas socks on!"

Foster turned in his seat and could just see a ring of bright red sequins below the cuff of Dad's trousers. He couldn't understand why, but it worried him.

"I couldn't get him to take them off," Mom clarified.

"Apparently!" Aunty said.

They were late, so everyone had already gone inside. Foster was about to get out of the car when Mom grabbed the back of Aunty's seat and leaned forward. She brought her mouth parallel to Aunty's ear and said, "You think this is funny?" There was a strange break in Mom's voice.

Aunty turned her head slowly toward Mom. Foster noticed that their noses were almost touching. He felt a tightness in his chest. He opened the car door and was about to slide out when he realized his seat belt was still on.

"Yes," Aunty said. "Yes, I do. And you had better find your sense of humor too."

"You two look like you're about to kiss!" Dad said loudly, unbuckling his seat belt.

Mom was halfway out of the car when she stopped and said to Aunty, "I know what you think of me."

"Maybe we should go home," Foster offered.

"Fossie, get out of the car," Mom said as she slammed the door.

The church was cool and dark and full of whispers. Foster could smell the old wood beneath his feet. He had on his good shoes, which clacked deliciously into the frigid air. He wanted to follow those little echoes all the way to the front and sit where he could see, but Aunty jostled him into a pew at the back almost immediately. Foster, taken by surprise, gripped the end of the row. It was so shiny with lacquer that it made a squeaky noise as his hand skidded along it. He was plonked into place by a hand on his shoulder, Aunty blocking all escape by taking the end position and dropping her handbag on the kneeler. Foster creased his face up and emptied his lungs like angry bagpipes. Aunty leaned over and said, "Come on, Fossie. Don't be a thundercloud."

His dad leaned across him then and said to Aunty, "Why are we sitting way back here?"

"Foster wants to."

"I do not!"

"No, he doesn't!" Dad replied.

"*Shush!* Both of you!" Mom said.

It had already started, but Foster couldn't hear a thing. The people looked small from back here. Not Pillow Top Mountain small, but smaller than usual. Someone was using a microphone, which only added shrill decibels to the already distorted voices from the apse.

Foster believed in all sorts of gods and wondered which one was responsible for putting fingers on babies. He'd never seen the finger of God, so he knew it was either really, really small or invisible. Seeing as how God would have to be pretty big to get around as much as he did, Foster assumed the whole hand of God was probably invisible. Like shrink wrap covering the leftover salad— you could only see it when the light hit it a certain way or if you wrinkled it trying to peel it off. The light in church was thick with colors, so Foster looked dizzyingly hard into the dark corners on the off chance God's finger would be in as much of a hurry as Dad.

"How *are* you? Nice to *see* you!" A lady sitting two rows ahead had spun around and fired an unforgiving whisper in their direction. It carried like water in a sieve, splashing into the spaces between people and causing some to startle and shift.

"Ruby!" Dad's voice, at a volume Foster recognized at

once as inappropriate, a volume Mom often described as "an outside voice" when Foster used it, hit the back of every head in the church like a bullet.

There was a short and distinct swishing sound as everyone spun around and then resettled. Mom placed her hand firmly on Dad's knee.

"No, it's me, Caroline!" the lady replied in a hissy whisper.

"Who?" The shifting and resettling of guests was unmistakably less tolerant this time. Some of the faces that turned lingered longer, and were like thunderclouds.

"Shush, Malcolm!" Mom said. Then she said to the Ruby-Caroline, *"Not now,"* with a desperate, pleading smile.

The Ruby-Caroline looked annoyed, as if she thought Mom was telling her off. Foster knew Mom wasn't meaning to tell her off. Even after the Ruby-Caroline had turned to face the front again, she occasionally flicked her head around and rolled her eyes in a harrumphing way.

"Wait! That's Caroline!" Dad bawled into the ceremony. Then he started to laugh. The sort of greeting-laugh you hear between grown-ups when they suddenly come across people they usually avoid and can't think of a way to get out of it. Then he said to Mom, equally loudly, "I've never liked her."

Aunty immediately got up and moved to the pew Ruby-Caroline was occupying. She scooched in next to her and started whispering in her ear. Half the room was looking at them all now. Foster was embarrassed. Mom was shoving Dad along the pew with her hip and Dad was getting angry. Foster had to anchor himself to his seat with one hand to avoid being shoved onto the floor. Mom leaned across Dad and hissed, *"Move, Foster!"* Foster began the humiliating slide to the end of the pew, feeling the way the Ruby-Caroline had looked. Though as she spun in her seat to have a look now, her eyes were snappy with smug curiosity. Foster felt sorry for her then, even though she seemed so pleased with herself. Foster sometimes did that—put on his pride face when he was really hurt. Sometimes withholding the show of hurt was the only defense left. And here was the Ruby-Caroline being told off *and* told she wasn't liked. She leaned over to Aunty and said something then that made Aunty look like she'd been slapped upside the head with a wet fish.

Aunty came back and pulled Foster to his feet with the same force she'd only just used to deposit him. She then leaned across and took Dad's hand to ease him to his feet. Dad looked confused and upset. Mom was sliding along the pew herself when she suddenly arced upward as if she'd sat on a tack, a resounding *Urrrgghh!* flying from her squared mouth as if she were the choir soloist. She had skidded into the puddle Dad had left behind.

Foster was burning inside and out as he watched Mom

ease her way over the slick spot. She caught herself mid-skid as her heel lithely slid through the urine that had dripped onto the floor. When she reached Foster, her skirt was wet.

"It's all right, Fossie," she said, resting her palm on his cheek. He realized then that he wasn't moving. His joints had locked. Aunty had already led Dad away, but Foster couldn't stop staring at the pee on the floor. He could smell it now too.

"You should know better!" An old lady had appeared from nowhere, like the finger of God, and had a talon-like grip on Foster's shoulder. Then she said to Mom, "Do you need any help, dear? It's all just attention-seeking, you know."

"No, thank you, we're fine," Mom said. She was easing Foster toward the door when it suddenly and sickeningly occurred to him that Mom was letting the old lady believe that he was the one who had peed. He looked up at his mom and felt a shame that rolled his bowels. He got ready to go out by himself, he made his own sandwiches, he picked up his toys. He didn't pee his pants. In that moment he hated her.

When they got home, Mom put Dad in the bath while Aunty put the kettle on. Foster sat on the floor in the hall just outside the bathroom door and listened to the calm talk and low laughter. It had been all quiet fury in the car on the drive home. Aunty had been angry at the Ruby-Caroline, which felt unfair to Foster. She seemed like a nice lady who just wanted to say hello. She didn't know Dad was going to use his outside voice in the most inside of inside places, and then pee himself. But Aunty fumed as she drove, occasionally spitting out half sentences in a kind of hiss-whinny Foster knew was the dead end of cranky.

"*Stupid* woman! If she'd just *shut* the . . . *Idiotic!* . . . told her *not* to . . . and you know what she *said* to me?"

"I think Linda's upset," Dad said to Mom. "Why are you upset, Linda?"

"She's not upset," Mom said.

"Yes, I am," Aunty said quietly. Then louder, "And why can't I be upset? Why are we all walking on eggshells around Malcolm? Why can't I be angry? He won't remember I've been angry anyway!"

"Mom, can I put the window down, please?" Foster tapped the window release energetically: frantic Morse code, no result.

"I didn't even want to go," Mom said. "You're the one who insisted."

"You can't just hide him away, for heaven's sake. He needs to get out," Aunty replied.

"Can I have the window down, Aunty?"

"Why is Linda upset?" Dad asked again.

"Besides, he had a good time. Malcolm, you had a good time, didn't you?" Aunty flicked her eyes to the rearview mirror before adding, "Oh no, he is sitting on a towel, isn't he?"

"It smells bad in here," Dad said. Aunty released the window lock and opened two windows halfway.

Foster used to be allowed in the bathroom with Dad. Now Mom said he needed privacy—which was strange because he'd just peed in a church. Dad used to tell some of his best stories while bathing. Foster would sit on the bathroom floor with his soldiers made cavalry by way of horses fashioned from toilet paper rolls and toothpicks. He would wage wars on the cold tiles, his horses carrying the injured back to the safety of a talcum powder beach. Dad had once told Foster that in terrible battles people sometimes lost their arms or legs, but would feel as if the missing pieces were still there.

"Can a man with no legs have itchy feet then?" Foster had asked.

"Oh yes," Dad had said. "It's called a phantom feeling. This is how remarkable your brain is, Fossie. It can re-create the feeling of something it knows should be there, but isn't. Your brain can fill in all sorts of holes. Make you experience things you thought were gone forever. Like telling a story."

Foster hugged his knees, his back against the closed bathroom door, and listened to his parents' voices on the other side. He imagined Dad's profile, half a face that looked a bit empty lately, and felt a stab of phantom feeling. A funny ache that told him the stories were still inside Dad somewhere, like an amputated foot that still itches.

"Fossie?" Aunty stood in front of him in the hallway. She held out her hand and said, "Well, we didn't get to stay for cake, did we?"

"Was there cake?"

"There's always cake." Aunty pulled Foster to his feet and gripped his chin between thumb and forefinger. Her hand smelled sharp and robust, like the cleaner Mom used on the kitchen sink. "So," she continued, "want to go get some cake?"

"Why did Dad pee in church?" He hadn't been sure he was going to say it until it was said. He had a feeling that it wasn't something he was supposed to ask at all. Nobody had mentioned it. Foster thought someone should at least mention it. He felt speaking it out loud had halved the thing already, and placed the blame squarely where it belonged. He could still feel the old lady's talons.

"He just got confused," Aunty said.

"Did he think he was on the toilet?"

"Sort of. It's nothing for you to worry about."

Mom had said that a lot lately too. *"It's nothing for you to worry about."* Foster found this response unsatisfying. It was the way grown-ups said they didn't want to talk about it. At least, they didn't want to talk about it with him. He knew they talked about it later, away from him, in places he used to be invited to and now was not. Like the bathroom.

"So," Aunty said. "Do you want to come with me for cake?"

Foster wanted cake very much, but he eased his face out of Aunty's fingers and said, "No."

When he got to his room, he slammed the door.

There was cake later. Aunty went and got it, and when she came back, the three of them—she, Mom, and

Dad—sat at the kitchen table and ate it. Foster cracked his door open just a bit, so it didn't make any noise. He could hear the rustle of cellophane and the clink of forks on china and the low voices, and no one came to get him. Even though he'd sent himself to his room, he felt the exclusion like an arrow.

Somehow it got to school. Someone had been at the church, some grown-up Foster didn't know. But that grown-up knew someone who knew someone who had kids, and all of a sudden Foster found himself on the receiving end of some peculiar attention he couldn't account for. Boys would sniff him as they went past and then giggle. There were some jokes about restricting fluids from the older boys. Foster laughed along at first because everyone else was laughing and he didn't understand. He didn't want to be kept outside the joke. He had been kept outside a lot lately, so if there was a joke, and people were laughing, he was happy to laugh along too. But then Jack, who got picked on a lot because he was smaller than everyone else and had a facial tic, told Foster, "They're laughing at you. They reckon you peed your pants in church."

"I *know* that, stupid," Foster replied. But he hadn't

known. The knowledge stung, but he wasn't about to worsen his humiliation by admitting he was stupid as well. "It wasn't me, anyway," he continued. Foster tried to sound casual and hoped his sudden breathlessness didn't make his panic show.

"Who did, then?"

"Dad. He's sick, you know."

"I thought he was just mental."

"He's not mental!" Foster said, thinking about the smell in the car. "He just got confused."

"About what?"

"Where he was." Foster turned on the tone Aunty used. Firm and instructive.

"Did he think he was on the toilet?"

"Sort of," Foster replied. "It's nothing for you to worry about."

"Not worried," Jack said. "Don't care. You're the one with the mental dad."

Foster was going to say something, but he couldn't think of anything to say that wouldn't make things worse. He was wretched about the whole thing. He concentrated on the cake he hadn't been invited to share, because it gave him something real to be angry about.

When they walked into class and sat down, Foster saw Jack lean over to Blinky and whisper in his ear. Then both boys turned around laughing, Blinky's eyelids fluttering like a bee's wing. Foster felt bad-dream breathless, made all the worse because he knew he was already awake.

Dad had once told Foster a story about a queen who was part bee and part lady. She had wings that beat so fast their thrum was like the ping of a harmonic on a guitar string. Her name was Melaina, a name Foster thought as musical as the sound of her trembling wings. She lived in the underworld, probably the same place Mom's moat snakes came from. Dad didn't actually say that, but Foster imagined the underworld to be full of dark things that trap princesses and inspire heroes. But Melaina was very sad. After dark she would take flight among sleeping humans and bring them a draft of honey laced with her melancholy. Dad said that's where bad dreams come from. And when she finished whispering her sadness into the ear of a soundly sleeping boy, she would leave a fine dust of golden pollen on his eyelashes, like a sticky gauze. That's why it's so hard to wake up from a nightmare, Dad said. She was not to be feared, but pitied. Dad sat on the edge of Foster's bed on the night of that story until he fell asleep again. Dad didn't sit on the edge of Foster's bed much anymore.

"Foster Sumner!"

Blinky and Jack were still looking at Foster, but so was the whole class now. Mr. Ballantyne was looking too.

"Yes?" Feeble, but it was the first thing to come out of Foster's mouth.

"Wakey-wakey, Foster, I said," Mr. Ballantyne continued. "It's your turn to give class news. What would you like to share this morning?"

Foster had forgotten about class news. Usually Mom helped him think of something to bring to class that he could talk about. Once he'd brought in a praying mantis the size of Mom's palm. She'd found it sunning itself on the kitchen windowsill and scooped it up, fingers kinked to gently tent the twiggy limbs. It had rocked back and forth on her hand, its huge head thrusting like a pigeon breast. Mom had put it in a shoe box with some leaves from the garden and said, "Now, that's news, Fossie."

But Foster didn't have any news today.

"I don't have any news today," he said. That was when he heard someone quietly say, "Oh, he's got news." Everyone started to laugh. Foster had to hold hard to that untasted cake to stop himself from crying. He hadn't cried at all, not really. Not even at the most terrible things, like Dad going missing or the church puddle.

"Settle down, everyone. No news at all, Foster? That's all right. Maybe next week." Mr. Ballantyne moved on to the next person, who had shells that used to be the home for living things. Sometimes the thing inside died, and sometimes it got too big and had to move into a bigger shell. You wouldn't know the shell had nothing inside unless you got right up close and gave it a shake.

By recess, everyone knew it was Foster's dad who had forgotten where he was and wet his pants, and although Foster was in the clear, so to speak, the snickering and nasty jokes continued. He began by laughing along with it all, as if he didn't care what they thought or said. But the laughing along didn't feel good, and Foster felt that if he laughed too hard he might break open. He needed something else. So from his sadness and his desperate need to hide from everything, Foster pictured his dad eating cake while he had to go to school. The result was anger. Foster decided his best way through the day was to join the ranks of the bullies against the real cause of his humiliation: Dad.

"It really stank!" he said, the small crowd around him beginning to grow. "I was like, 'Put the window down! Put the window down.'" Boys around him were shrieking with laughter. "Mom sat in it. She had it all over her dress . . . he just stood there like a baby. Mr. Wet Pants!" Boys echoed the phrase, a singsong slur bouncing off shiny concrete verandas.

"What'd you do then?" someone asked.

"Got out of there, stupid!" Foster said. Suddenly all

the boys were laughing at the stupid one who didn't know what Foster did then.

Soon the small gathering broke apart as boys headed to the after-school pick-up area. Still the chuckling and repeating of the story as smaller and smaller groups of boys hurried away to waiting cars, taking the news of the general's greatest lost battle farther and farther afield. Foster was now a part of the laughter instead of the object of it, popular by choosing the side of disgust over shame. He was one of the group again. It should have felt better than this. Foster couldn't understand why it didn't feel better.

Foster was the last one to be picked up. Mom was often late these days. As he waited, one of Jimmy Maher's friends spun past on his bike and called out, "Maybe next time he'll poo himself!"

Foster laughed hard, and waved. When he was finally alone, he cried. For the first time. He'd turned the tears into something else by the time Mom pulled the car up next to him, though.

Not-So-Nice Necessities

Foster didn't like it when Mom had a weekend shift at the meat factory. He knew she preferred nights to weekends because the money was better and Aunty was available, but she took the shift because she wanted to get ahead. That's how she explained it to Foster. "We need to get ahead a little," she said as she picked up the phone to call Miss Watson.

"Not Miss Watson," Foster said.

"Oh, Fossie, please," Mom said. "I know she's boring, but it's just for a few hours."

"Why do you pay her? She doesn't do anything."

"She keeps you safe," Mom replied. "Please, help me by not arguing."

The phone call to Miss Watson was always a long one, or at least longer than Foster thought it needed to be when Mom was only after a yes or a no. Miss Watson seemed to do most of the talking. Mom seemed mostly embarrassed and way too grateful. Especially since Miss Watson always came. Once again Miss Watson arrived within the hour. With her book.

She sat in the family room with Foster and Dad while Mom did those final little things she always did before leaving the house. There seemed to be more and more of those little things lately, and it all seemed a bit haphazard, as if she was delaying leaving until the last possible moment. She checked things twice, sometimes three times over: the back door lock, the kettle, the stovetop. She opened the fridge several times. She said "Yes, yes, yes" to herself as she did these things, then stood in the center of the room and smiled with a puffy sigh. Foster grew more and more anxious as Mom completed her little things before leaving. Every safety check was another step closer to him and Dad being left alone with Miss Watson.

Miss Watson had often explained Dad's demeanor after spending time with her as confusion and just missing Mom. "He's just missed you today, that's all," she would say when Mom would return home to find Dad pale with distress. He would be harder to settle, harder to distract. And Foster would watch Mom stare questioningly at Miss Watson as she shoved payment for her time into her knobby fist, wanting something from her other than what looked like judgment of her battle between necessity and guilt.

Being watched by Miss Watson was far worse for Foster than it was for Dad. Dad would forget. Dad lived in his right-now moment every moment. Foster often imagined it would be lovely to step into the next moment without the shadow of the previous moment following. He knew that feeling when he played with his soldiers or got lost in one of Dad's stories. But lately Foster found himself carrying his own distresses and the ones his dad had forgotten. So when Miss Watson eased herself onto the couch, book in hand, while Mom did her puffy-sigh last-minute reconnaissance of the house, Foster felt desperate. He grabbed Mom's arm as she picked up her purse.

"Miss Watson isn't nice," he whispered.

"Fossie, not now, please. Just do as she asks," Mom said, but Foster saw the creasing of her good eye where her mascara was smudged. Mom used to never go anywhere with smudged makeup. "We'll talk about it when I get home. I'm late." Mom leaned down and kissed Foster hard on the top of his head.

"Thank you, Miss Watson," she said, leaning over Dad and touching his face. "Malcolm, I'm off to work for a few hours. I won't be long."

"Okay," Dad said. "I'll wait here, then. Have a good day."

Then Mom was gone. Just for a few hours.

Bullying and Broken Things

Miss Watson opened her book and began to read. It was the same book she had brought last time. It wasn't a big book. Foster wondered if their family room was the only place she read. Dad was watching TV, his fingers stroking the fraying threads of the armrest as if he were reading Braille. Foster watched Dad's fingers. There was grace in them. Foster was about to go to his room and get out the general when Miss Watson said, "Turn off the TV. Go play in your room."

She didn't look up from her book. She waited just long enough to be sure Foster had not moved before casting her eyes over her spectacles and saying, "Foster, I said turn off the TV and go and play in your room."

"Dad likes the TV," Foster said.

"And I'm trying to read," Miss Watson replied, leaning forward and seizing the remote. She pressed a couple of buttons before landing on the right one in an irritated way. Then she tossed the remote onto the couch beside her. It took Dad a few seconds to register the loss of picture and sound. He turned to Miss Watson and asked, "Is it broken?"

"Yes," she said. "It's broken."

Foster stood, appalled and strangely frightened by this exchange. He wanted to go for the remote but instead stayed stock-still, powerless to do anything other than breathe a little faster and flick his eyes from Dad to Miss Watson and back to Dad.

"Now go to your room," Miss Watson said again.

"I'll play here," Foster said, but he didn't move and he had nothing to play with.

"You'll do as you're told or I'll tell your mom you've been disobedient."

"Can we get someone to fix the TV?" Dad said, staring at his reflection in the shiny black screen, his fingers rubbing the arm of the chair more firmly now.

"I'll get the soldiers, Dad," Foster said, resting his hand lightly on his dad's restless fingers. He was about to go to his room for the soldiers and clothespin basket when Dad stood up and said, "And I'll fix the TV."

Dad started toward the hallway first, then stopped and changed direction, heading for the kitchen instead. Miss Watson watched him disappear around the corner, then went back to her book. Foster contemplated following

Dad but felt it would be safer to keep an eye on Miss Watson instead. He couldn't explain the feeling. It was like making a choice between jumping off the starter's block at the swimming pool or lowering yourself slowly down the stairs. The depth of the water was the same, and if you didn't want to get wet, both choices were terrifying. Foster hated swimming.

The noise startled them both. Some banging and then something breaking. Foster got to the kitchen first and found Dad standing among thick shards of shattered china, opening and closing all the kitchen cupboards. He rattled plates around, got something out, and then closed the cupboard again, looking all gritty and sad, every movement staccato with imprecision. Hand extended, pulled back, knees bent, then straightened, like a strange hokey-pokey. Then he opened another cupboard and put whatever he had taken out back in. Always in the wrong place. Foster shadowed his dad, listening hard to the conversation Dad was having with himself. He seemed to be looking for something. He had just put some cans of dog food in the oven when Miss Watson appeared in the doorway looking formidable.

"What's all the noise?" she said, looking directly at Foster.

"Dad's looking for something."

"Mr. Sumner!" She said it so loudly that Dad startled

and let the oven door go. It sprang shut with enough force to rattle the shelves inside. "Sit down!" Dad did sit then, his eyes scanning the cupboards as if the answer to the question that would change everything was still inside one of them. Miss Watson sat at the table opposite him, splaying her book facedown in front of her before leaning forward and saying, "Get up again and I'll tie you to that chair."

"He wants to fix the TV!" Foster didn't know he was going to shout it until he had shouted it. Miss Watson went slightly cross-eyed with shock at the shriek. As she refocused, Dad said, "Is the TV broken?" and attempted to rise. Miss Watson rose too, leaned across the table, and smacked the back of his hand—a blow that landed Dad straight back in the seat of the chair. His face registered the sharp, stinging slap as if Miss Watson had taken a shard of that broken dish on the floor and ground it into his palm. Foster was stunned. It was the first time he had ever seen anyone slap a grown-up.

"Stop all this at once!" she said breathlessly, and for the first time looking out of control. Foster noticed her short breaths. She was a little bit afraid she had gone a little bit too far. Foster felt it and it gave him a little bit of courage.

"You stop it!" Foster shouted. "You told him the TV was broken and then he wanted to fix it and then he started to look for things to fix it but he forgot what he was looking for when nothing needed to be fixed at all because you're just a horrible lady!" Foster's throat hurt. The kitchen seemed a different color. They didn't shout in their house. Everything looked swimmy. Dad was rocking slightly, humming something.

"How dare you speak to me in such a way!" Miss Watson said.

"I'm calling my mom!" Foster wanted to stride to the phone with what little dignity he could still muster, but he found himself running instead. Miss Watson was scary, but she wasn't fast. She made a grab for him as he swung past her, but Foster outmaneuvered her by flailing one arm beyond her reach and changing direction unexpectedly. As he did so, a sharp triangle of sturdy china gripped the bottom of his shoe and sent his legs skidding out from under him. Foster landed hard on his bottom. Shocked, he sat there on the floor, trying to pull a mouthful of air.

"Fossie! You hurt?" Dad said, suddenly and inexplicably back from wherever it was he went lately. Miss Watson's fat-knuckled hand pinched Foster under one arm and pulled at him angrily.

"Your fault," she told Dad. "Bits of china all over the floor." But there was something beaten about the way she said it, as if Foster's hard landing had winded them both.

"Let's go watch some TV," Dad said, his hand resting on the top of Foster's head, then sliding down to cup his cheek. Miss Watson stayed in the kitchen. As Foster turned the TV back on, he could hear her sweeping up the broken dish.

When Mom got home, Miss Watson apologized for the broken platter, explaining that her attention had been stressfully divided between Dad and Foster after Foster became belligerent. Foster didn't know what *belligerent* meant, so he waited for a visual cue via Mom's facial expression. Mom looked at Foster in a frustrated, disappointed way, although she looked at most people that way lately. Even Miss Watson.

"The dish doesn't matter," Mom said. Miss Watson was still talking, but Mom's attention had been drawn to Dad, who appeared particularly fidgety and confused. He got up and walked into the kitchen, then walked back and sat down again, all the while turning his head this way and that as if to work out the direction of some unfamiliar sound only he could hear.

"Just trying to fix them both something nice to eat,"

Miss Watson continued. "It's just impossible to take your eyes off either of them!"

"I said it doesn't matter, Miss Watson."

"It matters to me. This is very stressful for me!"

"I'm sorry, Miss Watson. I won't ask you again."

"No, no," Miss Watson said quickly, the same hand that had slapped Dad gently resting on Mom's forearm. "I am happy to help any time you need me. This must be very difficult for you, Mrs. Sumner."

Miss Watson was heading toward the door as she said this, and it suddenly occurred to Foster that she liked coming over to watch him and Dad. Foster had thought that all her meanness and short-breathed snappy talk meant she didn't want to be here, but that wasn't true at all. She liked being here because she liked being mean. She was just a big bully. Foster felt satisfied at having worked this out and horrified that she'd be back, in equal measure. He didn't care about himself because he would always be able to outrun her, but he knew in that instant he had to protect the general.

He said it fast, sure that if he thought about it for even a second his courage would fail him altogether. "She hit Dad and I fell over!"

The effect of this statement, delivered in a hurried outside voice, was immediate and a bit funny to Foster. At exactly the same time, Mom and Miss Watson said, "What?"

They looked at him with the same expression too. Disbelief and shock. It was on now. Dad used to say that when battle lines were drawn between rivals of equal strength. Someone had to make a move. Foster knew it all rested on who looked at whom first. Mom slowly lifted her gaze to look at Miss Watson. Miss Watson's eyes flickered in Mom's direction, but she continued staring at Foster just long enough for him to know he had won.

"Miss Watson?"

"You can't possibly believe the boy," Miss Watson said. "He doesn't like you being away, so he's making things up. You need to get control of this one. Not an ounce of discipline in him."

"Miss Watson, did you strike my husband?"

"I had to get a little firm with him, that's all." Miss Watson made a slicing motion through the air with her hand, a gesture of finality and moving on, then attempted to land that hand on Mom's forearm again. Mom jerked herself away with a disgust more shocking to Foster than the slap in question.

"Get out of my house," she said.

Miss Watson opened her mouth to speak, but it took a while for something to come out. Foster found himself looking up at her with the same dropped-jaw uncertainty she was looking up at Mom with. Foster hadn't noticed the bristly hairs on her chin before. "I simply will not stand for this sort of talk," Miss Watson eventually said, gathering her face into a pinched scowl. Foster wanted to see her falter, weaken. He looked for it in the way she reached out for the door handle, the way she walked down the front path. But there was nothing. There was no give in her at all.

After Miss Watson left, Foster assumed Mom would want to put the kettle on and ask Foster exactly what had happened. He waited for it. But Mom sat on the couch opposite Dad and just looked at him. Her hands were shaking. She was squeezing them together so bits of them went white and then pink and then white again.

"Are you mad at me?" Foster asked.

"No. No."

Foster walked over and sat next to her. He wanted to kick-start this somehow, but Mom looked frightened. He wanted to tell her that the slap was only little, that Dad had probably already forgotten about it, that falling over wasn't all that bad. He wanted her to tell him that it was right to tell, that the telling of it hadn't just made everything worse. When her phone started ringing, Foster hoped she wouldn't answer it, but she began rummaging around in her handbag to find it. He heard the ringing get louder and sharper as Mom shoved things out of the way to clear a path to its squawking, and then it was in her hand, pealing over the TV that wasn't broken and Foster's next words.

"Are you going to put the kettle on?"

Mom stood up to answer the phone. She didn't just get up—she walked in circles in the kitchen and then sat and stood, and then walked down the hall and into her bedroom, closing the door behind her. She was crying. The last thing Foster heard her say into her phone was "Sometimes I want to hit him myself."

Earworms and Eavesdropping

Foster stayed on the couch opposite his dad and waited. He wasn't sure what for. He wasn't sure he wanted his mom to come out of the bedroom at all. At least not until she had stopped crying. He knew he was responsible. He could feel the hard edges of blame settling down inside him, like it would never, ever leave. He squeezed his eyes shut and tried to think of a story to tell. Nothing came. He thought about asking his dad to tell him a story, but Dad's stories didn't go so well lately. That wouldn't be quite so bad, but when the storytelling stopped, nothing else moved in to take over. Not even thinking. Dad had always had a thinking face, eyes that crinkled in a happy way as thoughts moved about inside his head. Sometimes it would still appear, but the stories that started soon dissolved into half-formed words and frozen hand gestures, leaving him as confused as everybody else about the strange wind that blew through, taking every word with it. Mostly his dad just looked empty.

Foster hadn't known that sometimes Mom wanted to hit Dad herself. He was sure he wasn't supposed to hear that. He didn't know how he knew this. It happened sometimes. He would hear things said by grown-ups—things said in quiet, shushed ways—and something about their bitten tone would make Foster feel guilty for having overheard. As if his ears had deliberately wandered the empty spaces between grown-ups, picking up stuff he wasn't supposed to hear. What was worse was that Foster was pretty sure these private things said into heavy silences were actually true things, truer than the careful sentences handed out to him. *It's nothing for you to worry about. It's nothing for you to worry about. Sometimes I want to hit him myself.* Foster had a feeling he was being lied to all the time. Being told it was nothing to worry about didn't make the worry go away.

Foster knew other true things he kept to himself. He knew Mom was not a princess scarred by magic; she was an ordinary woman wearing her brain injury like a party mask, courtesy of a drunk driver. He'd heard Mom say that on the phone to someone once. She'd been crying then too. That was when Foster realized that truth often comes with crying, so when grown-ups are crying, you should pay close attention to the stuff they don't want you to hear. Especially if you're the one who made them cry.

Mom came out of the bedroom and went to the bathroom. Dad started humming something Foster recognized. When Mom eventually appeared in the doorway, the humming had really taken off. Foster had joined in.

"What is that?" she said. "I know that song."

"I don't remember the words," Dad said. "But I like it. What song is it?"

Mom wandered to the kitchen, humming herself.

"Now I've got an earworm!" she said, smiling.

"Earworm!" Dad said.

"Earworm! Earworm!" Foster said. He was smiling too. He could make things right now. He could distract Mom, just like she distracted Dad when he got confused or upset. Mom was putting the kettle on. Finally. They were all humming, Mom throwing in a few la-las as well. Foster took Dad's hand and led him to the kitchen table, then stood in front of the kettle. He liked to watch the kettle water roll about. He could see it through the window on the side. That was when he noticed Mom pouring herself a glass of wine in a long-stemmed glass shaped like a closed flower. He was glad. That always distracted Mom too. And made her happier.

Foster was annoyed when the doorbell rang. They were all having a nice time at the table like they used to.

He could imagine a story being not very far away. He imagined Dad beginning just the way he used to, with a *"Nowwwww"* that was long and full of secrets, followed by an *"I don't know if you know this,"* which always meant a new thing about to be told. With the three of them sitting around mugs of tea and hot chocolate, just like they used to, just imagining a soon-to-be-told story was enough to satisfy Foster. Then the doorbell. Stupid old-fashioned thing that looked like a bigger version of a bike bell. You had to turn the paddle and a mallet ran around the inside of the bell dome striking pins, sending a shrill metallic rattle to bounce off every person in the house. Mom jumped before saying "Why doesn't she just knock?" in an irritated way, and Foster knew Mom knew who it was. She set another cup on the kitchen bench before going to open the door.

"I bloody hate that doorbell," Aunty said as she strode into the room.

"Why don't you just knock?" Foster said.

"Cheeky!" Mom said.

"But you said—"

"Why don't you go and get ready for bed?" Mom said.

"I haven't finished," Foster said, gripping the sides of his mug.

"Well, take it with you," Mom said. That was when Foster knew true things were going to be said at that table.

He wasn't allowed to take drinks from the kitchen into other parts of the house unless they had lids on them. Like water bottles that Mom sometimes poured juice into. She was funny about spills lately. Even with Dad.

Foster slid off his chair and did his best saunter toward the hall, leaving his mug on the table in what he hoped was a statement of his displeasure. Mom didn't seem to notice.

"Hi, Malcolm!" Aunty said, leaning over his dad and kissing him on the side of the head. Dad smiled his warm smile.

"Didn't know you were popping in, Linda. Why didn't you tell me she was popping in?" he said to Mom, who was making Aunty a cup of tea, her back to Dad.

"I didn't know," she said without turning. Foster knew she was lying and it irritated him. Mom was keeping secrets from Dad, secrets other than wanting to hit him. He strolled out of the kitchen and into the hall, meandering in a way that usually wound Mom up something awful when she had asked him to do something like go and get ready for bed, but again she didn't notice. By the time she looked up to see if Foster had left the room, he had hid himself just out of view in the foyer beyond the hall. He could hear Mom settling Dad into the lounge chair he spent most of his day in, turning on the television, turning up the volume, and placing Dad's mug on the table beside him. She must have been planning to say things more important than the spill risk from either of them. Dad had scalded himself once on a cup of soup. It was bad enough that Mom had to get a tube of cream from the pharmacy. After that, she always stuck her finger in Dad's hot drinks before serving them.

From where Foster stood he could peek into either room, but he didn't dare.

"This tea isn't hot," Aunty said.

"Sorry. Habit."

"I think you should call the police," Aunty said.

"Oh, for heaven's sake. That's just what we need. An escalation response."

"She assaulted him!"

"I'm all right now. If I'd known you were going to react like this, I never would have told you."

"Oh, I'm so glad *you're* all right now."

"That's not fair. I have so little time to actually *feel* anything. I just react, react, react all the time. Trying to stay on top of everything. The other day I found food stashed in weird places all over the house."

"So what? Pick your battles. Let him hide some food."

"Some of them were dairy products."

"Oh." Aunty paused before saying, "Don't ask for my help if you don't want my help. Don't tell me my brother got slapped by *your* babysitter if you don't want me to respond to that. If you want to look after him and everything else all by yourself, then don't complain to me about it."

"You don't understand!" Foster could hear the fogging up in Mom's voice. She was crying. It gave him a pain in his throat. He wanted to march in there and defend her. He wanted to tell her that he had seen Dad hide the milk and had wanted to put it back but it had frightened him. That hidden milk had been a burden to him, but he figured that if it stayed hidden, no one would know or care. He hadn't expected it to start smelling like it did.

"What is it that I don't understand?"

"It's just that"—Foster heard Mom take a deep breath—"you see, he used to look after me. *He* looked after *me*. You weren't around much for that, so you don't understand what this is like for me." Foster heard Mom's telling-off voice in that last bit.

Foster's every sense was so intently concentrated on listening to the conversation and remaining undetected that he didn't notice Dad coming up behind him until it was too late. Dad's outside voice bellowed, "This is cold!" cracking the vault of Foster's focus so unexpectedly that he screamed and spun around. He caught Dad's mug of tea with one flailing arm, slapping it out of Dad's hands, splashing tea up the wall, and sending the mug spinning across the floor.

"Foster!" Everyone was suddenly standing around him, looking down at him, their shock at the commotion coming together into a tight knot of angry faces. Even Dad looked angry, and it was all his fault.

"Foster! Have you been listening?" Mom wasn't crying now. She'd dried up fast. Now she was yelling. "What are you doing here? I told you to go to bed!"

"Everyone calm down," Aunty said. "It's just a bit of tea."

Foster felt all that unresolved church pee indignity roll just like the kettle water right up to his eyeballs.

So he screamed back. "It's not my fault! I didn't do anything!" He ran down the hall to his room. Before he slammed the door on the three startled grown-ups, he added something he hoped would hurt his mom good: "And I knew about the milk!"

Apples and Anger

It was the third time Mom had forgotten to make Foster's school lunch, and Foster didn't want anyone to know because it embarrassed him. He didn't have any money either. He sat cross-legged on the lawn with the others as they peeled open their sandwiches and sticks of stringy cheese, and he turned down the offer of an apple from someone he hardly knew out of hard pride. He wanted to be able to tell Mom he hadn't eaten all day.

Foster didn't care about school much anymore, so it didn't matter to him whether he ate or not. He liked the misery of feeling hungry, always thinking it would distress his mom more when she heard about it than it did him when he was feeling it. Dad was always very particular about school lunch. Mom said if Dad was so particular he was welcome to make it for Foster himself. Dad said that a good lunch on school days made Foster's brain work better. If his brain worked better he would learn more, and learning was the key to good stories. Foster no longer cared about learning or stories. Watching all the learning and stories shatter like broken glass inside his dad, when his dad had been having good lunches all his life, made Foster feel like he'd been lied to from the get-go. This morning his dad couldn't remember why he was sitting at the kitchen table, even though his toast was right in front of him. So much for decent meals. Still, Foster sat in the car all the way to school waiting for Mom to remember to give him some money for lunch, and then felt both crushed and satisfied when she drove away leaving him with nothing.

Foster had his grump on—what Aunty called a puss face—and as a result the handful of friends he usually wandered around with had quietly detached themselves from him and his grump. Since he was generally a well-behaved boy, at first his occasional naughtiness in the classroom and on the playground earned him some status as a smart-mouth. The other kids liked a smart-mouth just about as much as his mom and teachers hated one. It was new to Foster, so he started by pushing the small boundaries: he was late to class even though he'd been dropped off on time; he said he'd forgotten his reading book when really it was shoved in the bottom of his backpack with a few pages torn out for good measure. Then, as his friends became bored with the small stuff, Foster grew in confidence. He developed a dull-eyed broodiness and began answering every question asked of him, at school and at home, with "I don't remember." It seemed to work well for Dad.

Mom hated "I don't remember" more than anything else. She was particularly annoyed because Aunty seemed to enjoy it. Aunty would laugh when Foster would turn to her, full of nervous swagger, to say, "I don't remember." She would chastise him, but Foster could tell her heart wasn't in it. She was too giggly. And when she told Mom to pick her battles, which she said a lot lately, Mom would walk out of the room.

So between Mom's rage and the teacher's disappointment and Aunty's enjoyment, Foster found himself getting lots and lots of attention. Almost as much attention as Dad.

Aunty was around more lately. Mom was taking on extra shifts. Foster heard her telling Aunty it was just until Dad's pension was released, just until she was approved for a carer's allowance, just until there were some services in place. "Just until, just until, just until . . . ," Aunty said. Aunty always said she didn't mind looking after Foster and Dad, but her "I don't minds" came with comments that even Foster could smell the criticism in.

Mom and Foster weren't home long from school, a drive Foster had spent torturously alternating between angry silence and a repetitive singsong performance of "I haven't eaten all day," which he had been rehearsing since he turned down that apple.

"Foster, make yourself something to eat," Mom said.

"You make me something to eat."

"Please, Fossie. You are quite capable of making yourself a sandwich."

"I don't remember how."

"Puss face," Aunty said, and laughed. "I'll make him a sandwich."

"Don't you dare." Mom had been fussing about, peeling off jewelry and dropping it on the kitchen table, when she stopped suddenly and said it. Her fingers were still poised at one earlobe, about to remove an earring. Foster knew Mom must have been out to see people today. She only ever wore her jewelry when she was going out to see people, and they were always people connected with the "just untils." Aunty looked bewildered for a moment, then her face settled into the bemused expression she wore most of the time in their house.

"Oh, pick your battles," she said.

"I'm picking this one. The last thing I need on top of everything else is a perfectly capable child reverting to a sulking, attention-draining baby."

"Of course," Aunty replied, "because you've got a husband already doing that."

"How dare you!" Mom walked across the kitchen to the fridge, never taking her eyes from Aunty. She got out a bottle of white wine and poured some into a coffee mug.

"Don't you have to go to work?" Aunty asked. "Isn't that why I'm here? Because you need to work *just until*? If you're not going to work, if you're going to sit here and drink and take yourself this seriously, I'll go home to my dog."

Foster sat at the table. He was invisible again. He raised his arms and began swinging them from side to side. Like a drowning man. Like one of those sports fans he saw on the TV.

"Why are you always criticizing me?" Mom said. "You make things more difficult! Just like Fossie! Why is everyone making everything more difficult for me? Foster! What are you doing? Put your arms down!"

"I haven't eaten all day," Foster said, arms rigid in the air.

"Look," Aunty said, peeling the coffee mug out of Mom's fingers, "you go and get ready for work. I'll make a sandwich for Fossie, and then if you want me to go home so you can do all this by your humorless self, I will. You don't want help with the doctor, you don't want help with the accountant, you don't want help with social services—you just want me to appear on demand and suck up my

118

own fury that my brother will suffer the more you suffer. And you *are* suffering. Because you don't want help."

"I have to get ready for work," Mom said. Aunty's eyes had drifted until she was no longer looking directly at Mom. Both Foster and Mom noticed and followed her gaze. A shaft of sunlight had fallen into the house, straight through the foyer that led to the hall. It shouldn't have been there. That light was all wrong, and within seconds they all realized why.

"The front door," Mom said as she was running.

They caught Dad at the mailbox this time.

Foster was very little when Mom had her accident. She didn't actually have the accident herself. Someone else had the accident and messed her up in the process. That was how Aunty described it, anyway. Someone had messed Mom up in her car. Foster's only knowledge of messes on the road was those street sweepers they sometimes got stuck behind when they were driving. The ones with the big round brushes that would spin and spin right up against the curb, sucking the lunch wrappers and cigarette packs up into the truck's wide belly. Foster liked the noise they made and would strain in his seat to try to get a better view. Mom would get irritated when she was stuck behind the sweeping truck. She would always say, "Why are they cleaning up the road at this time of day?"

One day Foster had said, "That's what happened to you, Mom, isn't it?"

"What do you mean, Fossie?"

"Aunty said you got messed up on the road."

"Did she, now?"

Foster didn't have a lot of clear memories of that time. He knew Mom hadn't come home for a long time and Dad had looked after him for a long time. Not unlike what was happening now, Dad had become distracted and depressed and had taken a lot of time off work. There had been other people around, but Foster couldn't remember who they were. He remembered going to the hospital and being plonked onto a hospital bed beside someone he didn't recognize—a big, ugly doll with tubes and wires growing out of it—and then being given an orange juice in a silly plastic cup that was difficult to drink out of. Actually, he didn't know if he remembered that or if he had been told about it. Dad had said that he spilled that orange juice. Everyone had found that funny. Just like Dad's spills were funny at first, Foster supposed.

Foster didn't remember missing Mom. There was an awareness of her being gone, but always the assumption that she was coming back. Time was vague—it had washed off him like bathwater going down the drain, bathwater Foster knew would magically appear the following night as if it had never left.

When Mom had eventually come home, she had had a walker and the different face. Foster didn't remember Mom using the walker. He only remembered Dad putting him on the seat built into it and giving him rides around the house while Mom was sleeping. Sometimes strangers would come to the house, strangers who were not quite guests but something else or something more. They had used slow, loud voices on Mom and fast, quiet ones on Dad.

Dad had told Foster lots of stories when Mom came home. At night when the TV had been turned down low and only left on for the flickering light it provided, Dad would make up all sorts of adventure stories, his face appearing and disappearing in the irregular illumination. Foster couldn't remember most of them, but he really liked the one about the Amazing Human Brain, a superhero like no other. He had asked for that story again and again. It didn't matter how injured the Amazing Human Brain was or how much it forgot how to do— it had an unparalleled strength that clawed back everything that was lost. Change was fuel to this superhero. The Amazing Human Brain thrived on it. Even with all these changes, everything would ultimately settle back into its proper place. Mom was home. The bathwater kept appearing.

Everything about Mom had gotten better and better, except her face. Dad had told Foster she had worked very hard to get everything back. Foster wasn't sure where everything had gone in the first place, but Mom's ability to get it all back just confirmed for Foster that change didn't have to be bad, and it didn't have to change him.

These days the strangers who came to the house used the slow, loud voices on Dad and the fast, quiet ones on Mom. The strangers started coming after Mom and Aunty had the fight that ended with them corralling Dad at the mailbox and wrestling him back inside the house. And it was a wrestle. It brought Miss Watson out of her house. Dad was yelling as if he didn't know who Mom and Aunty were. Foster thought it was funny until Mom started to cry. Miss Watson stood on her veranda, blood-red concrete on limestone pillars, as if she were a statue on a plinth. Her mouth was a tight line and she looked very disapproving but somehow satisfied.

That was when Foster started hearing the word *services* a lot. At first he thought they were going back to church, and he made the decision right then and there that if they were, he wasn't going with them. But as the word continued to be used and no one asked him to put his good clothes on, he realized this must be some other kind of services. The services turned out to be the strangers.

This time in the midst of strangers and busyness, there were no walkers to ride, no stories to be told. Foster watched Mom become a whirling dervish, but there was no devotion in it. Dad said a dervish was always devotional. Mom just looked panicked and tired.

123

Foster had come to believe that people who went away came back eventually, even if they looked a bit different when they climbed back into themselves. The slow erosion of this conviction was making him panicked and tired as well.

Sausage Rolls and Strangers

The morning the two services strangers came for the meeting, Mom cleaned the house more thoroughly than usual and put on a dress she usually wore only when she was going out. She also arranged her hair in a pretty way and put makeup and jewelry on. Foster didn't know why, but somehow the wearing of a going-out dress inside the house made this morning more important than other mornings. Foster waited in suspense for some sort of instruction, some direction on par with the appearance of lipstick and earrings. He was really irritated when the only thing Mom said to him was, "You'll have to play quietly in your room for a while this morning."

"Why?"

"Because I asked you to."

"Why?"

There was a loud knock on the door then. Aunty had taken a screwdriver to the doorbell and disabled it because its rattling bellow seemed to set something off in Dad. He'd get all antsy and start wandering around the house looking for tools. Mom had hidden all his tools. They used to sit on the bottom shelf of the laundry cupboard in red tins shiny as fire engines, but had to be hidden away when Dad started taking the doors off the kitchen cupboards while Mom was in the shower.

"I'll get it!" Dad called. Mom followed him to the front door and they returned to the kitchen with Aunty. Aunty placed the large cardboard box she was carrying on the kitchen table. Foster could smell the warm pastry immediately.

"I asked you to pick up a cake!" Mom said.

"Well, I got sausage rolls," Aunty said. She looked Mom up and down, then said with a slight smile, "I see you want to look like you're coping."

"Can I have a sausage roll?" Foster asked.

Mom looked Aunty up and down. Then she said, "You could have made a bit of an effort."

"This is me having made an effort. *And* I brought sausage rolls. As far as effort is concerned, I'm exhausted." Aunty kissed Dad then. He clapped his hands and rubbed them together.

"Let's have sausage rolls!" he said.

"I want one too," Foster said.

"Not yet," Mom said, retrieving a large platter. "When they get here. Foster, you can take some to your room."

"When who gets here?" Dad asked.

"Nothing for you to worry about," Mom said.

"Why do I have to go to my room?" Foster asked.

"The social workers are coming, Malcolm, remember?" Aunty said.

"I don't want anyone in the house today," Dad said. He looked sullen and annoyed. "Why wasn't I told about this?"

"You were told," Aunty said. "They won't stay long."

Mom arranged the sausage rolls on the platter, flakes of buttery pastry sticking to her fingers, delicious-smelling slivers crumbling onto the table. She was muttering, like she did a lot lately, but Foster still heard it: ". . . asked you to bring cake . . ."

Foster was picking up pastry crumbs with a wet finger when there was another knock at the door.

"I'll get it," Aunty said.

"No, I'll get it," Mom said. "Fossie, go to your room."

"Why do I have to go to my room?" Foster demanded, somewhat soothed by Aunty shoving three sausage rolls wrapped in a paper towel into his hands.

"Foster, I have no idea," Aunty said. "But just do it. Make Mom happy, huh?"

"I'm going with him," Dad said, reaching over and grabbing sausage rolls with both hands.

"Actually, I think it'll make her happy if you stay," Aunty said. They could hear fast, quiet voices in the family room. Foster took his bounty and headed down the hall. Halfway to his room, he stopped. Without thinking too much about it, he walked back and stood just out of view in the foyer. With his hands full, he used his mouth to manipulate one end of a sausage roll into it. Chewing slowly, he peeked into the family room.

There were two of them: a man and a woman. The woman was very thin and wore a skirt that stretched tight as a drum across her thighs, so tight he doubted she could have crossed her knees. She had her ankles crossed instead. She was running her palms across her lap, smoothing the skirt. The man was fat. He was fat all over in the way Foster imagined jolly people would be fat. He wore a suit and tie. The suit jacket had no chance of ever being buttoned and Foster could tell the tie was too short. Dad would never wear a tie that short. The man seemed to have bosoms as well. Foster stifled a giggle with a swallow.

They were soon joined by Aunty and Dad. Then Mom walked in, placing cups of tea and coffee on the little table usually covered with dirty dishes and magazines, now polished to a high shine. She had to make several trips to bring in all the drinks, then the sausage rolls. She put the sausage rolls down as if she was sorry about them. Foster heard her suck her tongue into a *tsk*.

"Thank you for coming," Mom said. "This is my husband, Malcolm. My sister-in-law, Linda."

"Linda," Fat Man said, leaning forward to shake Aunty's hand. "Malcolm," he said, leaning forward to shake Dad's. Fat Man's hand was left hanging awkwardly in midair before it was retracted. That was when Foster saw that Dad still had two fists full of sausage rolls. Mom reached across to take them, but Dad pulled his hands away roughly and said, "Get your own! Plateful there!"

Mom sat again, looking uncomfortable.

"Don't blame you, Malcolm," Fat Man said. "I love sausage rolls." With that he picked one up and took a hearty bite.

Thin Lady said, "We understand you have a ten-year-old son? It would probably be useful if he sat in on this. Get some understanding of where things are going?"

Foster didn't want to give Mom the opportunity to make excuses for him not being there, so he stepped out of hiding right away and said, "Okay."

Mom looked uncomfortable again, as if she were about to take a test.

But Dad smiled his happiest smile and said, "Hiya, Fossie!"

Candor and Contradiction

They stayed for an hour. Foster watched the clock hands crawl around the face, wishing he had gone to his room and refused to come out. His boredom for the duration of that crawling hour trumped all his previous annoyance at being left out. Dad was bored too. Foster could tell, because he got up several times without excusing himself and wandered off. Even Foster knew not to do that. Aunty would go after him and bring him back, and even though Thin Lady said it was quite all right if Malcolm wanted to go and do something else, Mom got a bit bothered by that suggestion, so the regular Dad retrievals were put up with for her comfort. Foster thought they should just let him go take some doors off or something.

They talked a lot about Mom getting enough help and enough rest and about setting things in place now for when things began to deteriorate even more. Aunty asked about residential care, which elicited a surprisingly fervent "No, no, no, no" from Mom, along with a hurried but firm explanation that that sort of thing was surely a long way off. Aunty took pamphlets anyway. Foster whiled away some of the time flicking through them, looking at pictures of well-dressed, happy old people doing crafts and playing board games. It occurred to Foster that there were no people in the pictures like Dad. No one wearing a suit.

Soon the sausage rolls were gone. Foster and Dad kept shoving them down. Foster waited for a scolding word from Mom about ruined appetites, and was surprised when she didn't seem to care. She was all high-strung, as Aunty called it, because everyone was finding talking directly to Dad hard work. When they did ask him a question, he'd answer the one that was in his head rather than the one that was in the room. So Mom did a lot of answering for him, which Foster thought was a bit rude. She wasn't giving Dad enough time to think, and she was making him look stupid. The only time Foster was really interested in what was going on was when Fat Man asked him a question. Foster was really annoyed when Mom started to answer for him as well.

"Foster is doing just fine. He's been very good, very understanding and—"

Foster flicked all the pastry crumbs sticking to his

clothes onto the floor and said, "You said I was making things more difficult."

"Oh, Fossie, I did not," Mom said with an embarrassed smile.

"Yes, you did. Remember? You said Aunty was too. Didn't she, Aunty?" Foster waited for Aunty to come to his aid.

Aunty hesitated before saying, "Well, not exactly. That's a bit out of context."

Foster didn't know what context was but continued anyway, speaking right at Fat Man, who had asked the question after all. Mom didn't even know how Foster was doing. It's not like she asked him.

"I miss Dad's stories. Mom is angry a lot. She never cooks really good stuff anymore. She works a lot. And I have to watch Dad when he used to watch me."

Foster felt a bit breathless when he finished speaking. Mom looked devastated.

"That's in context!" Aunty said, laughing.

"That can't feel very good, Foster," Fat Man said.

"It's okay."

"Do you want to talk more about that?"

"No."

"Are you sure? Because we can talk about that if it's bothering you."

"Not bothered."

"Well, let's look at it this way. What's one of your favorite things that Mom used to cook?"

"I don't remember."

"Sure you do! What's your favorite thing to eat for dinner?"

"I don't remember."

"Oh, for crying out loud!" Mom said, suddenly standing up. The whole room snapped to attention. Foster had been enjoying the chat with Fat Man, and had been planning to drag it out a bit longer. He felt very visible in the spaces between each of the questions Fat Man asked. Every eye in the room had been on him, and not in the sideways way people usually looked at him lately. That sideways look that was really just a way of estimating his distance from a grown-up conversation so that the volume could be adjusted to exclude him. But Mom had all the attention now, and for someone who had just stood up and yelled into a quiet room, she was looking as if she didn't want it anymore.

"What's wrong?" Dad asked.

"Nothing. Nothing, Malcolm. I'm just going to take these cups out." She quickly placed the empty cups on the platter. One fell over.

"I'll help you," Aunty said, leaning forward to stand up the cup.

"I don't need any help."

"You don't say."

"Foster, perhaps you could go and play now," Thin Lady said. "Let the grown-ups talk for a bit?"

"I'm going with him," Dad said. "Who are you people, anyway? When are you leaving? I don't want you here."

"The kitchen's that way," Aunty said, pointing. Mom was still standing in the middle of the room, platter in her hands.

They all started moving then, all at the same time. Mom to the kitchen, Aunty right behind her, Dad down the hall, Foster right behind him. In a matter of seconds, Fat Man and Thin Lady were left alone in the room, everyone else having scattered as if on the tailwind of a fart. Dad used to say that whenever a room cleared quickly. Foster thought it was funny.

"Are we on the tailwind of a fart, Dad?" Foster asked, taking his dad's hand.

"I did fart," Dad said. Foster laughed until his tummy hurt.

The signs went up the following day. Mom printed them on the computer in big, bold lettering—all in capitals too. They said things like *LAUNDRY* and *KITCHEN* and *BEDROOM*, and there wasn't just one of each. One went on the door of the room, and one went on the wall of the room in case Dad went in there and then forgot which room he was in. In the kitchen there were lots of signs. *CUPS* and *SPOONS* and *PLATES*, and on the fridge door a sign that said *MILK, BREAD, BUTTER*. Mom suggested Foster do drawings on the signs. Pictures of what the signs meant, or just nice colored borders to make them more interesting. Foster was thrilled to be included and was hunkered down at the kitchen table doing just that when Dad joined him. Foster spread the pencils out so Dad could reach them. Dad didn't say anything, he just picked up a pencil and began writing numbers all over the sign that read *TOILET*.

"What are you doing, Dad?" Foster asked without looking up.

"Making money for other people," Dad replied.

Aunty had been suggesting signs around the house for a while, but Mom didn't do it until the respite lady suggested it. Aunty was mad about that and had told the respite lady that Mom was pig-headed. Foster wasn't supposed to have heard that, and Mom hadn't heard that. She had been at work. Respite Lady had told Aunty, "We are all on the same side here." Aunty had told Respite Lady she had a dog who was easier to communicate with.

Respite Lady's name was Sophie. There were a few different ones, but Sophie came the most often. There was only one respite man and Dad didn't like him. Dad thought he was Mom's new boyfriend.

Foster asked Sophie what respite was. She said it meant giving Mom a break so she could go out shopping or see a movie. Foster waited and waited for Mom to take him to a movie. She didn't. Foster felt like she was respiting from him as well. He didn't know where she went when she had her respite time, but she was always dressed up and always seemed to come back even more tired. He assumed she was still working on her "just until" things.

"Let me come to the accountant with you," Aunty had said one day. "Let me help you get the paperwork together. What else do they need to get this thing moving?"

"It's our private financial business," Mom had replied.

"Then talk to Sophie! Talk to anyone! Get some independent counseling on this compassionate grounds pension release thing!"

"I am."

"From whom?"

"It's nothing for you to worry about."

"You are getting completely lost, you know that?" Aunty had said. "You are so desperate to be in control of everything that you're just white-knuckling with no direction at all. Being a guilt-ridden martyr doesn't make you noble. Sure as hell won't save Malcolm either."

Mom always drank wine after Aunty had visited.

Foster knew what a martyr was from Dad's stories. It was someone who would rather die than give up what he or she believed in. In ancient times people did it a lot. Foster didn't know whether to be fiercely proud of Mom's allegiance to Dad or terrified that it would kill her. He wasn't afraid of her getting lost, though. She'd been lost before and clawed her way back. Foster was hoping she'd drag Dad back with her this time. Foster assumed the signs around the house were a part of that.

Dad had been getting confused in the house quite a bit. He knew he was home but kept asking why things had been moved or changed. He became convinced that his favorite chair had been sold and replaced with another.

He was sure the carpeting in the hall had been ripped up and replaced, and demanded to know where Mom had found the money to do that. He could go hours and hours without speaking a word and then become really angry that all the clothes in his wardrobe had been swapped with someone else's. Foster didn't like this angry Dad, and Mom just seemed to make things worse. When she called him irrational, Dad would slam doors and try to get away from her.

Sophie told Mom that Dad was not being irrational, that his delusions were as real to him as they were unreal to her. She suggested distracting Dad rather than arguing with him.

"Can we tell him his old chair is out for cleaning and will be back tomorrow?" Aunty asked. "He'll have forgotten about it by tomorrow, and if he hasn't we can just tell him the same thing again."

"I will not become a part of his delusion," Mom said.

"You already are," Aunty said. "He thinks you're sleeping with that guy who comes in on Tuesdays." Then Sophie told Mom to pick her battles, which Foster knew would really set Mom off.

Sophie also suggested a name tag: something Dad could wear on the off chance he wandered away while they were out or left the house without their knowledge. Mom did her "No, no, no, no" thing again, assuring Sophie that the need for a name tag was a long way off. Aunty got mad again because she'd been mentioning that for a while herself. Mom suggested a card placed discreetly in his wallet until Sophie pointed out that a stranger would be reluctant to go through Dad's wallet, especially if Dad was already in a distressed state. Something more immediately and visually apparent would assist in the police being called promptly. So Sophie suggested a nice piece of jewelry—a bracelet or pendant—with Dad's name and a couple of phone numbers on it.

"Malcolm doesn't wear jewelry," Mom said.

"Teachers at school wear a plastic thing around their neck when we go on field trips," Foster said.

"I'm with Fossie on the lanyard," Aunty said.

"Fossie, this is nothing for you to worry about," Mom said.

"I think he is worried," Sophie said. "I think he should be encouraged to contribute and to understand what's happening."

"I don't think a child should have to deal with adult issues," Mom replied.

"I think you might be forgetting that he is already dealing with it," Sophie said.

"I haven't forgotten anything," Mom replied.

"But you did!" Foster yelled. He'd had a yell in him for a while, just sitting there festering, a yell he'd done in his head, a yell his clothespin-basket captives had done for him, a big yell about missed lunches and silent dinners and all the anger that hid under even the nice things that were said around here lately. "You forgot everything! Dad told me. But you got everything back after you were cleaned up! And now Dad's been cleaned up too, and you're just mean about it and everyone's always mad! And if he runs away again I'm going with him, and we won't wear lemon yards!"

"Lemon . . . yards," Aunty said slowly.

"Lanyards?" Sophie offered.

Foster ran out of the kitchen and down the hall to his room, trying to make his feet really loud. He heard Mom call after him pleadingly. He heard her sorry voice following him. He didn't care. He stood on the threshold of his bedroom and yelled, "Pick your battles!"

Then he slammed the door.

Dog Collars
and
Day Care

Foster hadn't felt really scared until Dad forgot Geraldine. It wasn't that Dad sometimes forgot her and then reconnected when she shoved her wet snout into the palm of his hand. Dad just suddenly stopped recognizing her altogether and started shoving her out onto the street as if she were a stray who had somehow managed to get into their backyard. Geraldine started hiding down in the back by the jacaranda as if she somehow knew Dad wouldn't venture that far. But there was always that random moment when she was sunning herself on the bricks by the back door that would be interrupted by Dad's furious conviction that she didn't belong to them. If Dad could completely forget the years of burying his face into her prickly muzzle and holding her like a baby on his lap, how long would it be before Dad tried shoving Foster out through the side gate? Geraldine had been around longer than Foster too.

Mom put a padlock on the side gate, but that just meant Dad started dragging Geraldine by the scruff through the house and pushing her out the front door.

"No, Dad!" Foster would say.

"Stay back, Fossie. We don't know if it's trained to attack or not."

The problem was made worse by their inability to keep a collar on Geraldine. Twice she'd been picked up by the dog pound man. Mom was dumbfounded by how Dad managed to get Geraldine out of the house so often without her knowledge. A neighbor would bring her back, or once a police officer brought her back, and neither Mom nor Foster had even realized she was gone.

Mom tried showing Dad photographs of Geraldine and photographs of Dad with Geraldine. Dad enjoyed that and talked affectionately about her. But when confronted by the living beast, Dad could not connect the dots. She was no longer his Geraldine.

Sophie suggested trying to introduce Geraldine as a new dog, a devoted companion for Dad. The problem was that by the time they had decided to try this plan, Geraldine had acquired some new behaviors of her own. She would see Dad and run for it. She even stopped coming inside the house when Mom invited her—something she ordinarily loved to do—clearly associating that with being dragged across the floor, legs akimbo, and unceremoniously booted onto the street. Geraldine got wise, and Mom got desperate.

"I thought pets were supposed to be comforting," she complained to Sophie.

"This is unusual," Sophie responded.

"There's a whole dang science behind it! Geraldine should be reducing his anxiety, not making it worse," Mom said.

"Yup," Sophie replied. "Maybe I'll cancel pet therapy."

Pet therapy was a part of Dad's new Day Program. The way Mom, Aunty, Sophie, and Mom's new "boyfriend" spoke about it, Foster just knew it had capital letters and was very important. Dad was to go out with Sophie twice a week and spend a few hours socializing. This was to give Mom and Aunty more of a break and to offer Dad some "Stimulating Activities in a Homelike Environment." That was what it said in the pamphlet. Foster thought the whole thing was a bit odd, because Dad had never really liked socializing. And if pet therapy was a big thing there, they had better be prepared to lose some animals.

They all went to see the Homelike Environment with Stimulating Activities together. Sophie had suggested it might be nice for everyone to go and visit and see what it was like. Dad was particularly compliant that day, which made getting out of the house easier than usual. There was only one trip back into the house when Mom realized

Dad was wearing two pairs of trousers. He accused her of doing it but still let her lead him inside to remove the outer pair.

For the first time, Dad had to wear a lanyard. It was only temporary while Mom organized a nice silver chain for his wrist. She had ordered one with chunky links and a blank disk from a catalog. Foster had helped her choose it. Mom said she would get it engraved later. Foster thought the lanyard looked very professional, though, and secretly hoped Dad could keep wearing it even when his bracelet was ready. It had his photograph, his name, and two phone numbers on it. It looked just like the ones teachers and even doctors wore. In very small print under Dad's name was written "Memory Impaired." It swung on a thick purple strap from Dad's neck like a credential.

As soon as they started driving, Dad began reading out every road sign he could see. Foster joined in. Foster was excited when Dad began the game. It was one of their special things, and he found himself really happy for the first time in a very long time.

But this time Dad wasn't doing it right. Sometimes he just kept saying the same word over and over again. When he did say a sentence, it didn't carry on from Foster's the way it was supposed to. Sometimes Dad called out another word before Foster had even finished making up his sentence.

"Dad, you're not doing it right," Foster said impatiently.

"Stop," Dad read. Then immediately, "Stop! In the name of love."

"We're not doing songs," Foster said.

"Stop! In the name of love."

"Stop!" Foster said.

"In the name of love."

"Mom!"

"Fossie, does it really matter? Just let him do what he wants."

"But there are rules! He's ruining it!"

"Fossie, please! He doesn't even know it's a game. He's not even playing with you."

Foster looked at Mom aghast. It wasn't just her tone, which was rude and impatient. It was her saying out loud what Foster already knew but was pretending wasn't true so he could have this small moment of enjoyment with Dad. *"He's not even playing with you."* Foster felt that same Big Shops humiliation roll over him like a tractor wheel.

"Speed hump," Dad said. *"Hump* means 'sex.'"

They spent the rest of the drive in silence.

Locked In, Locked Out

When they arrived, Sophie was already there. She must have been waiting with her nose pressed to the window, because she walked out and across the parking lot before Dad was even out of the car. Foster thought she looked more excited about this visit than any of them were.

In the car, Dad had kept on making vague references to sex that Foster didn't really understand, but he was pleased to see left Mom in a knot of agonies. He knew what a penis was, but the other words were mysteries. His only clue that they were inappropriate was Mom cranking up the car radio and then talking loudly over it about nothing.

"I don't know if this is a good idea today," Mom said immediately to Sophie.

"Oh, just come in and have a look around. Malcolm, you want to have a look, don't you?"

"Don't know where I am."

"He's not quite himself today," Mom said.

"All the more reason," Sophie replied. "Distraction, distraction, distraction." She said each word with a pat and squeeze of Mom's forearm.

"Where am I?"

"Day care, Dad," Foster said deliberately. Mom hated the Day Program being called day care. Foster had heard Aunty calling it day care and it had started a fight with Mom. Aunty had said she was just trying to be funny. Aunty hadn't been invited to come with them today.

"It's *not* day care," Mom said.

"Well, no," Dad replied. "Fossie's too old for day care. Isn't he? How old are you, Fossie?"

"Not my day care, Dad. Yours."

"Fossie!" Mom performed an almost perfect pirouette in an effort to tell Foster off face to face, but he skulked behind Dad, avoiding her eyes. He knew he had her because she was dressed like she was coping again and wouldn't want to give that up.

Sophie was already leading them toward the big glass doors. They opened automatically onto a large room with a long reception desk on one side. The desk had flowers and pamphlets on it and a sign framed like a picture that read WELCOME. THIS DESK IS TEMPORARILY UNATTENDED. Dad read it out loud.

"Yahtzee," he said.

"Yes, we don't have to bother about that," Sophie said. "Come through."

Farther on was another set of doors, but these ones didn't open automatically. There was a keypad on the wall next to them. Sophie pressed some of the buttons and the doors opened with a *swoosh*. Foster could immediately smell that same sharp, lemony abrasive cleaner Mom used at home on the sinks. Somehow it made him feel more comfortable. As soon as they were through the doors, Sophie pressed another button and they swooshed shut.

"Why is the door locked like that?" Foster asked.

"We have security here," Sophie said. "Just so staff can enjoy time with the clients without having to constantly head count." She finished off with a laugh. Clearly she was trying to be funny. Mom hadn't laughed yet.

They went down a long, wide corridor with floor-to-ceiling windows that looked out over atrium gardens with benches and ponds. There were rooms to the right. Some had beds in them. But they didn't stop until they got to another set of double doors at the end of the hall. This one had a sign on it that read DAY PROGRAM. Foster had been right about the capital letters.

Inside was a calm busyness. Like the rallying point for school fire alarms, but with old people. Really old people. Most people were doing things, or being encouraged to do things. Jigsaws, painting, board games, Yahtzee. Dad was good at Yahtzee. Foster tugged on Dad's sleeve and pointed.

Dad pulled his arm away from Foster and took a step toward Mom.

"When are we going home?" he asked.

Sophie was talking, had been talking continuously, about what they did and other services they offered. There was counseling for clients and their caregivers, cooked lunch, activities designed to work with and improve upon the skills and cognitive abilities of each client. Also, and perhaps most importantly, the opportunity to meet new people and keep up social skills that could sometimes be lost in the more isolated care situations. All this as they wandered around the room peering over shoulders and smiling at strangers. Foster noticed that the clients didn't smile much. He also noticed that Mom wasn't smiling much. Not real smiling, anyway. Just a lip twitch when a staff member smiled at her. The memory of a response.

"Why do you call them clients?" Foster asked. Mom cast an eye at him. She could really cast too. Foster felt the hook of it. He was embarrassing her.

"Well, a client is a person who needs a service that we provide," Sophie said.

"I know what a client is," Foster said. "My dad has clients, and they don't look like this."

"Foster!" Mom said.

"When are we going home?" Dad asked again. "I have clients to call."

"Well," Sophie continued. "There are all sorts of clients and all sorts of services. For example, your dad can come here for just a couple of hours to watch a movie, or he can come for the day and do all sorts of different things. Whatever he wants."

"Or he doesn't have to come here at all. He can stay at home with us," Foster said.

"Oh, Fossie, please stop," Mom said.

"It's all right," Sophie said reassuringly to Mom. "It's a huge adjustment, and no decision has to be made right away. We just want to provide you with options and support."

"I appreciate it," Mom said. "I really do. It's a lot, you know? I'd like to bring my sister-in-law to have a look if that's okay?"

Foster was stunned. He looked up at Mom and could see she was quite sincere. But she hated Aunty. They were always fighting. Aunty was always upsetting Mom and leaving the house annoyed and muttering. He couldn't explain it, but he felt like he was losing a bit of footing.

"Of course that's okay," Sophie said. "I was half expecting her to come with you today."

"You're not leaving me here, are you?" Dad asked.

"Not today, Malcolm. Let's go home for now." Then she said to Sophie, "It's a beautiful facility."

"Well, it's here for you," Sophie said. "Come, I'll let you out."

Sophie walked them back the way they had come, all the way to the keypad door. As she pressed the special numbers, Foster said, "If you have to be let out, you're a patient. Mom was a patient once."

Swoosh.

Tilting and Taking Sides

Of all the social workers and home aids who came into the house, Foster liked James the most. James was New Home Aid Man. They'd had to get rid of Old Home Aid Man because Dad wouldn't let him in the house anymore.

Dad had been asking Mom about her boyfriend for a while. In keeping with Sophie's *"distraction, distraction, distraction"* line of attack, they had all ignored it and talked about something else. Aunty had even gotten Mom to have a bit of a laugh about it. No one knew Dad was brewing a rage. It wasn't real, after all.

Old Home Aid Man had arrived as usual on a Tuesday morning. Foster had never seen him before, but it was school vacation. The most boring school vacation he'd ever had. So a visit from a stranger was at least a temporary, hopefully entertaining, diversion for Foster, who spent most of his time stuck in front of the TV with Dad.

When Mom opened the front door, Dad had stood up immediately. Old Home Aid Man went to shake Dad's hand, but Dad kept his hands at his sides, fingers coiled into fists.

"Why are you here?" Dad said quietly. "What are you doing in my house?"

"Malcolm?" Mom said. "Malcolm, you know—"

"Your boyfriend? Yes, I know all about your *boyfriend*."

Foster had been dumbstruck by Dad's tone at first. It was nasty. Foster had never known his dad to say or do anything vicious, so he had been immediately frightened by this unrecognizable thing coming out of the person he loved. It had taken a few seconds for the sentence to slowly untwist itself until it rang like an echo inside his head.

It had taken less than a minute. Dad had started roaring at them, saying they were having an affair. Foster didn't know what an affair was. Then Dad lunged forward. Mom screamed. Foster slapped his palms over his ears and wanted to squeeze his eyes shut, but he couldn't. He just kept watching, all the while listening to the distorted mishmash of muffled bawling, coming from who knew where, mixed with the blood pounding in his ears.

Old Home Aid Man was smaller than Dad, but he was fast. He blocked Dad's flailing fists with his arms and at the same time managed to get a solid grip on Dad's wrists. Then he firmly pressed Dad up against the front door. Foster gently released the pressure on his ears. All the screaming had stopped.

Old Home Aid Man was speaking softly, gently, "There you go, Malcolm. It's all right now. Ease off. There you go. I'm going to let go of your wrists now. Can I let go of your wrists now? There you go." He slowly allowed Dad's arms to drop to his sides, but kept a loose hold of them. It looked like they were holding hands. Then Dad began to cry. Foster felt a stinging in the back of his throat and swallowed hard.

"Mrs. Sumner, are you okay?"

"Yes," Mom said. That was when Foster realized she had been crouched on the floor. Foster had missed her ducking to avoid getting hit, but the thought of it then seemed very funny. He didn't want to laugh, though. Almost as much as he was determined not to cry.

Mom took Dad by the hand and sat him back down. Dad looked wretched.

"Please don't leave me," Dad said.

Old Home Aid Man sat on the arm of a lounge chair, where Mom said you weren't supposed to sit, and watched Dad and Mom. Then he touched Mom on the shoulder before walking outside. He made a phone call from the driveway. Foster watched from the family room window. While Old Home Aid Man talked into his phone, he glanced occasionally at the house.

By the time Sophie arrived, Dad had calmed down. It was as if it had never happened. Except it had. Sophie had brought James with her. As soon as Sophie sat down, Foster whispered, "I think that man hurt my dad."

Sophie stroked the top of Foster's head and said, "No, I don't think so. I think everyone is okay." Then to Dad, "Malcolm, this is James. He's a friend of mine. I was hoping he could watch TV with you."

"I need a shave. I've got to get to work."

"No problem," James said. "I'll give you a hand."

As they left the room, Dad said, "Who are you?"

"I'm James."

"James! For goodness' sake! I haven't seen you in years. How've you been?"

Sophie had brought some paperwork in a file with her and asked Mom a lot of questions. Was this the first time Dad had become violent? Were his responses to being upset or confused changing? Did Mom feel she and her son were unsafe? All three questions followed one after the other with unfilled pauses between, pauses Foster assumed were supposed to be filled with answers from Mom. But she was quiet. She just sat in a chair swinging her legs as if the chair were too big for her.

Sophie had to lean forward and touch Mom's wrist to get a response.

"No, no," Mom finally said.

"No to which question?" Sophie asked. "Shall I start again? Would you like a cup of tea?"

"Foster, go and play in your room," Mom said.

Foster did go and play in his room. It was one of the few times he actually didn't want to hear what the grown-ups were saying. He had to think about things first. He had to not cry.

Dad used to talk a lot about positions. Financial positions, political positions, legal positions, ethical positions. The word *position* became fascinating to Foster, far more so than the word preceding it. A position was clearly an important thing. Foster would listen to Dad talking on the phone after dinner, listen to him arguing a position or sharing a position, and without asking for a definition, Foster was pretty sure he had worked out the gist. He had to have a position. He wasn't sure why he felt he had to have one, or even what his position would be, but he knew what a position was and that having one would take away the awful fidgetiness in his chest.

Foster remembered the first time he had ever taken a position and won with it. It was a school night, and when Mom told him to pack up his drawing and get ready for bed, Foster said no. Mom was accustomed to

Foster's delay tactics and bargaining for more time, but he could see she was unprepared for an absolute refusal. She laughed a little as she said, "What did you say?"

"I said no."

Dad was interested now. He looked up from his laptop and said, "Why would you say that?"

"I'm taking a position," Foster replied.

There was a brief pause before Dad started laughing. Big delight-riddled guffaws. He wasn't laughing at Foster. Foster could tell. Dad seemed genuinely interested when he said, "What are you taking a position on, and what would that position be?"

"I'm taking a position on bedtime," Foster replied solemnly. "And my position is that I'm not tired, so I will draw for fifteen more minutes and then go to bed without a story to make up the time."

Foster waited and watched Mom and Dad looking at each other.

"I can't argue with that position," Dad said. "That is a reasonable position, well expressed."

"Okay," Mom said. "Fifteen more minutes, no story." She didn't seem as delighted as Dad, though. Foster felt the win of the position like a free-wheel bike ride down a big hill.

"However," Dad said, "having people respect your position is far more likely if you talk with them about it. Respect their position too. No more answering Mom with a no, okay?"

As Foster sat in his room rearranging his soldiers he thought about his position now. He thought about Sophie's questions to Mom, because she would be answering them and he didn't trust what she would say. She was the one who wanted to hit Dad sometimes. Would Mom tell Sophie that? Would Sophie write that down? Dad just wanted a man he didn't like out of his house. Foster had thought finding a position on this would be easy. He felt he must have one ready even if he was never asked for it. It would stop him from getting lost in everyone else's. He didn't want Dad swinging at people, but he didn't want Mom on her knees on the floor either.

Foster carefully placed the general under the clothespin basket on his pillow. He could hear Dad and James laughing in the bathroom. He suddenly realized that having a position really just meant taking a side.

Temporary Tattoos

"They're all so old," Aunty said. "Did you see anyone there even close to Malcolm's age?"

"No. And yes, I know," Mom replied.

"I still think it's the right thing. You can't cocoon him here. It'll drive you both insane. And with this sort of help, you can get back to some sort of normal life."

"Normal life?" Mom asked.

"You know what I mean. This is it, right? This isn't temporary. It's not going to get any better. And having him registered for this will surely make it easier when you have to start considering some sort of residential facility."

"That's nothing for you to worry about," Mom said. "That's still a long way off."

"Oh, for heaven's sake!" Aunty said. "That's your bloody mantra, isn't it? Will recent behavior have any impact on . . ." Aunty didn't finish the sentence, just sort of tapered off into a wary head cock in Foster's direction.

"I haven't done anything!" Foster said.

"No, of course you haven't, Fossie," Aunty said quickly. "No one's talking about you."

No one talked about him much at all anymore. Even when he was naughty. Mom and Aunty were just back from visiting the Day Program—Aunty for the first time—and James had just left. Mom had left Foster behind with Dad and James this time. Foster knew why, but nothing had been said. He almost wished it had been. He would have felt better had he received a bit of a lecture in the car on the way home last time. But still there was this carefulness around him, this unwillingness to waste emotion or energy on him. There was such a shortage of energy in everyone lately that Foster could hardly generate a sour look with deliberate rudeness.

"You talking about Dad's behavior, then?" Foster asked.

"No, Fossie," Mom said.

"Yes, you are."

"It doesn't matter, Fossie. Go and play."

"Does so matter," Foster said. "You almost got messed up, Mom."

Aunty started to laugh quietly.

"That dog's in the yard again!" Dad called out. "Better call someone! Who do you call about something like that?"

He was standing at the kitchen window. They were all

in the kitchen with him, so Foster wasn't sure why he was yelling.

"I've already called the police," Mom said. "They'll be here soon."

Mom hadn't really called anyone, but the lie was good for all of them. James had explained that to Foster. He said they weren't really lying to Dad, they were just telling him a story. Like Dad used to tell Foster stories. Telling Dad a story was sometimes kinder than arguing with him and making him upset. So Foster didn't interrupt with truth anymore when he heard Mom tell a lie.

Foster liked it when James came around. There were others who came. Sophie, of course, who was all smiley business. She was nice, but there was something about that smiley business Foster thought was a bit phony. She probably had that face everywhere she went. There were a couple of others on an unpredictable rotation whose faces Foster could never quite remember once they had left. They were just hands and voices and efficiency. But Foster really liked James.

James was younger than the others. Foster had heard Mom complaining to Sophie about his age. Not in a bad way, but with the same fretful voice she used with and about other people she thought were too young to be doing what they were doing: the girl who served her at the shops, the boy who came to fix the leaky toilet. James was short too, and had a curlicue of piercings that went from his earlobe all the way up and around to the top of one ear. Most were studs, but there was one small gold hoop that James would sometimes spin when he was talking.

"Can I get my ear pierced like James?" Foster asked Mom.

"No," Mom said. "You're too young and it's not nice."

"I think it's self-expressive," Foster replied.

"I don't even want to know where you heard that. Find another way to express yourself," Mom said. "Draw a picture or something."

James had told Foster that body art was a form of self-expression, just like anything else we do to show people more about who we are. The stories we tell, the clothes we wear, the things we create. James was particularly impressed with Foster's stories—the ones Dad had told him so many times he had memorized them, as well as the ones Foster made up. James encouraged Foster to make up more. Sometimes they would sit together—Dad, James, and Foster—and Foster would tell a story. Foster wouldn't always know where the story was going to go, but James said that didn't matter. That it was actually a good thing. That the only thing that mattered in any story was what was happening in the moment of it being imagined. If

Foster got stuck, James would ask him a question to push him forward, and he always remembered where Foster had left off if they had to wait a day or two to continue it. Foster began to look forward to James's visits more and more.

Foster thought Dad liked James too. Of course, it was hard to tell what Dad really liked, but Foster thought it was a good sign that even though Dad still didn't like strange men in the house, he had never taken a swing at James. James never called Dad sweetheart like some of the other helpers did, and rather than stand over Dad to talk to him, James would sit cross-legged on the floor in front of him. Foster would join them and nod along, and between the three of them it felt like a real conversation was occurring, even though James did most of the talking.

One day Mom returned home to find all three of them—Dad, Foster, and James—sitting cross-legged on the floor, applying brightly colored temporary tattoos to each other. James had brought them with him because the story they were continuing with was about ancient warriors who decorated their faces and bodies before going into battle. Foster ran to Mom feeling strong and happy, proudly presenting his motley arms for inspection.

"Look at my woad!" he said excitedly.

"Your what?" Mom met the moist onslaught with a combination of disinterest and irritation. "You're all wet, Fossie," she continued, peeling his arms away from her body. "James, clean all this up before you leave."

Then she went to make a phone call, her position clear.

Distraction by Design

For as long as Foster could remember, he and Dad had celebrated their birthdays together. Their birthdays were only one day apart, and Dad said that Foster had been the best birthday present he had ever received. Mom would decorate the house with balloons and streamers, and Foster would invite his school friends. Mom would invite some family—the only part of the whole thing she really didn't like. It was the only day of the year Foster would see these family people. He didn't know who they were, only that they stood in a small group slightly separated from everyone else, as if clinging to each other. They'd have a few drinks, shake Dad's hand, and then leave.

Foster's excitement about his birthday would usually begin to bubble about two weeks beforehand. Mom and Dad would start making sly references to it, little teasers. Foster would get wide-eyed with anticipation as Mom began planning the nibbles and cakes. There were always two cakes—one for Foster and one for Dad. Foster had the ice-cream cake and Dad had the one with lots of booze in it. Dad would watch Mom slapping the batter from one side of the bowl to the other and say "Come on! Fill 'er up!"

A lot of the family people would have left by the time Mom lit the cakes and dimmed the lights. She would put the cakes next to each other, and Foster and Dad would line up behind them, Foster heel-toeing as if preparing for a sprint. They always blew out each other's candles. Foster didn't know why exactly, only that it was a tradition. And Dad said tradition was very important.

So when the birthdays were two weeks away and Mom hadn't said anything or even bought any invitations for Foster to hand out, Foster began to get nervous. There was increased interest in his birthday party at school this year. Boys Foster had not even intended to invite began coming up to him and asking when it was going to be, which he thought was strange. But he answered them all with the same gusto, promising ice-cream cake and invitations any day now.

Foster waited as long as he could. Then the week before, feeling as if he would burst with the anxiety of non-preparation, he asked about it at dinner.

"Mom, what day are we having our party?"

"Oh, Fossie. We need to talk about that."

"Are we having a party?" Dad asked.

"Yes, Dad. For our birthdays. Remember?"

"We'll talk about that later," Mom said.

"Is it our birthdays already?"

"Next week," Foster said, looking at Mom with a scold in his eyes.

"Malcolm, is that dog in the yard again? Better check," Mom said.

Foster couldn't believe it. He stared at Mom for the longest time, but she wouldn't meet his eyes. He couldn't believe Mom was using Geraldine as a distraction. They weren't supposed to do that. James had said so. They weren't supposed to encourage the things Dad got wrong. They were supposed to ignore them and move on to happy things. A party is a happy thing. Dad had left his seat at the table and, leaning on the kitchen sink, was surveying the backyard. Foster knew right then that Mom was trying to trick them both on purpose, and it made him very angry.

"Don't see it," Dad said. "Do you think it's out there?"

"What shall we eat, Dad?"

"When?"

"At our birthday party," Foster said, anger turning to bravery.

"Is it our birthdays already?"

"Foster, that's enough," Mom said. "I promise we'll talk about it later."

"Pizza!" Foster said.

"And red sausages!" Dad said.

"For now, let's just eat dinner," Mom said. Then she leaned across and placed her hand on top of Foster's, saying, "You will not get what you want by using your dad to manipulate me."

"But you did!" Foster said, breathing a bit faster, anger turned to bravery turned to fear. "You used Geraldine. You're not supposed to do that," he finished quietly, looking down at his plate.

"Who's Geraldine?"

"Malcolm, sit down and finish dinner."

"And cake," Foster said softly.

"Two cakes!" Dad said, returning to his chair. Mom reminded him to eat again, so he picked up his fork before continuing. "Always two cakes, right, Fossie? You blow out mine and I blow out yours."

"Tradition," Foster said. But the excitement was gone. The excitement of a party, the excitement of besting Mom, the excitement of two cakes, all twisted up now into a funny, sick feeling. Foster understood that having no party was taking the position of defeat, taking the side of everything being changed forever.

They ate in silence. Well, Foster and Mom did. Dad ate

with the sounds in his head. The sounds he often mumbled along with. There was a time when Mom would have asked Dad what he was saying, or what he was hearing, but not anymore. Dad just became frustrated that no one else could hear what he was hearing, and Mom became frustrated that Dad was hearing things that weren't there in the first place. Once when Mom was feeling particularly sensitive to the muttering, she turned on the TV as a distraction. They couldn't see it from the kitchen, but they could hear it. That didn't last long, because Dad went into a frenzy thinking there was someone else in the house. He jumped up from the table and crept around with a frying pan, convinced they had an intruder. It took ages to calm him down, even after Mom turned the TV off.

Foster liked the tiny, squeaky sounds Dad made. They were like a fairy language: the thrum of wings spinning around dragon eyelashes. It meant Dad was still telling stories on the inside. Foster could relax into the rhythmic hum and trill of Dad's small noises, but Mom always got to a point where she dropped her fork loudly and deliberately on her plate.

"Malcolm, can you please just eat!" she said.

"What have you done to my food?" Dad asked. Foster noticed the plate was still nearly full.

"Nothing," Mom said. "I haven't done anything to your food."

Dad shoved the plate away. Dad's plate shoving wasn't as impressive as it used to be. Before Mom started putting his plate on a rubber placemat, Dad had been able to skid that thing right across to the other side of the table, where it would slide into Foster's own with a hardy *chink*. That had always made Foster laugh.

"Poison," Dad said.

Foster had finished his dinner and noticed a thick, untouched piece of sticky, glazed meatloaf still shimmering on Dad's plate.

"Can I have that?" he asked.

"No, Malcolm. It's not poisoned."

"You're trying to kill me."

"Mom, can I have that piece?"

"No one's trying to kill you."

Mom stood quickly and began collecting plates. Foster watched as she scraped Dad's meatloaf into the trash and dumped the dishes into the sink.

"Why are you doing this to me?" Dad asked. Mom stood stock-still where she was, staring out at the jacaranda. Without turning around she said, "Hey, Malcolm, we should talk about the party for your birthdays."

"Is it our birthdays already?"

Red Sausages and Shame

Foster spent a long time making Dad's present. James helped him. Foster had done all the hard stuff. He had written the story and drawn the pictures, but James had bound it with stiff card and split pins so it looked like a real book. The way James had bent the card made it open like a real book too. Then he had helped Foster glue the cover picture onto the front so that it was straight and fitted properly. Foster had spent the most time on the cover picture. Writing the story had been easy. He had been telling it and acting it out on Pillow Top Mountain for months. James had just helped with some spelling. But the cover was particularly important. Dad had always said book covers are what draw us first to a story, like smiling eyes in the face of a stranger. Foster had looked at lots of the covers of Dad's books to see what sort of smiles Dad was drawn to, and then created his own cover with all the elements of color and design most likely to draw Dad in.

Then he wrapped *The General,* first in tissue paper, then in bright red wrapping paper left over from Christmas. There was birthday wrapping paper, but Foster's general wore red.

Foster didn't show it to Mom. He wanted it to be a surprise for her too.

It was going to be a small party this year. Foster was allowed to invite five friends instead of his usual ten, but he didn't mind. Mom was cutting way back on guests too. It seemed to make her happy to do so. "Let's keep it short and not fill the house," Aunty had said. Aunty wasn't usually involved in organizing the party, but this year Mom seemed grateful for the interference. Mom struggled more with her guest list than Foster did with his. But Aunty said if Dad asked about anyone not there, they could just introduce the same person to him twice as different people. Mom didn't find that as funny as Aunty did.

Foster and Dad were in charge of the balloons and streamers. Foster told Dad what to do, including how to make the fart noises with the balloon necks. Mom tolerated that, but when Dad let go of a balloon that flew through the air like a coil of flatulence and came to rest with a slap in Mom's hair, she wasn't very happy. She had arranged her hair over her bad eye for pictures again.

Dad was having a good time. As people arrived, Aunty

stood next to him while Mom answered the door. Sometimes she linked arms with him. Once she held his hand. Foster couldn't understand why he felt uncomfortable. There was something in the air. A quiet that didn't quite belong with balloons and streamers. It wasn't that people weren't making any noise. It was that the people making it seemed immediately apologetic about it. Greetings were punctuated with an awkward hush. Laughter was bitten in half. And when Dad said "Look at all the presents! Is it Christmas?" nobody laughed at all.

Foster couldn't wait for the present opening to begin. It was the first time he could remember being more excited about what he was giving than what he was getting. There were some big presents there too. He looked around for his friends and saw them all standing in a knot around the red sausages. He walked over. That was when he heard it.

"Which one's the crazy one?" Oliver asked.

"That's his dad over there," Blinky said, pointing.

"He doesn't look crazy," Charlie said.

"He's not," Foster said. They all turned to look at him.

"But you said he was," Louis said. "You said at school."

Foster had said it. He stood there, between red sausages and shame, remembering all the times he had joined in at school to shift the target of the teasing from him to his dad. He'd had a brief respite when another boy's dad had gone to jail, but somehow that had ended up giving the boy an unexpected standing, and Foster's crazy dad had quickly been reestablished as the bigger disgrace. Foster tried to think of a way out, but all he wanted to do was cry. He tried to casually reach for a red sausage, but it came across as more of a snatch.

"It's an illness," he said.

"Your dad thinks it's Christmas. That's crazy," Oliver said. Everyone laughed.

Foster was so full of things to say that he couldn't squeeze a single word out. He was like the sauce bottle in the fridge when it got that drip booger crusting the opening. He would squeeze and squeeze, knowing the bottle was full, until eventually the contents would explode from the tip, always on an angle so that sauce shot across the room and he got in trouble for making a mess. He was pretty sure if he said anything right now, it would be that messy.

Lately Foster had been able to turn off his sadness. It used to be that his sadness was a noisy thing. That breathing while choking on mucus and tears produced a racket. But lately he'd been able cry without tears even spilling out. His eyes would get a bit fat, and just as his lashes would begin to get wet, the tears would disappear. He'd watched himself in the mirror. It was as if he could suck them back in, drain them back to where they came from.

Sadness returning to sadness's origin. It was in his face, though. All that noise he reabsorbed would flush out his skin terribly and make him shake. His soundless crying could be very noisy indeed. He knew he was wearing that face when he saw Mom looking at him from across the room.

He walked away from the red sausages as Mom started to walk toward him. She had just settled Dad into a chair. He had been quite excited when everyone was arriving but had since quietened in a way Foster recognized. He was getting confused. He was looking frightened. Aunty was sitting on the arm of the chair, where Mom said you weren't supposed to sit, with her arm around him. Dad was picking at the threads in the upholstery.

"What's wrong?" Mom asked. She intercepted Foster in the hall, her hand on his shoulder. "Where are you going?"

"To my room to get a game for us to play."

"Oh, okay. I thought you looked upset."

"No."

"Well, don't be too long. You wanted this party, so your friends are your responsibility."

Foster nodded. He waited for Mom to turn and walk away before running to his bedroom and shutting the door. Then he dragged the table next to the door across, just enough to prevent anyone from being able to open it.

He knew he would get in a lot of trouble for that, but he didn't know what else to do with his feelings.

"Your friends are your responsibility." Foster knew he was responsible. He was responsible for what they thought and what they said, because he had thought it and said it himself. For all the times his heart was under the clothespin basket with the general, there were just as many times he had chosen saving himself over defending his dad. Foster lay down on his bed and imagined never having to leave his room again.

On with the Show

At first he thought the raised voices were just party voices. But only for a moment. Foster pushed himself up onto his elbows and stared at the back of his bedroom door, trying to untangle the sounds he could hear from the hall. They were far away at first, but then closer and closer to his bedroom door. They weren't happy sounds. It was yelling and pleading, which was okay because Foster had become accustomed to yelling and pleading. But private yelling and pleading was different from putting on a show for friends who already thought Dad was crazy. He crawled off the bed and moved quietly toward the door. He didn't know why he was doing it quietly, because no one would have been able to hear him over the noise on the other side. He pulled his table back and wrapped his fingers around the door handle. Just as he was turning it, he heard Dad, right on the other side, ask, "Who are they? Why are they here?"

Foster carefully opened the door. Dad was standing with his back to him. Mom was halfway down the hall looking a bit wild. At the end of the hallway, in a swarm that spilled out into the kitchen, were party guests. Drinks in hand, bobbleheads zigzagging for a better view—and in the middle, Aunty trying to steer people toward the front door with her phone wedged between her ear and her shoulder. Oliver waved at Foster awkwardly as he was maneuvered out of sight, Aunty's hand firmly on his shoulder. Foster heard her opening the front door.

"I know what you're trying to do," Dad said. "I know what's going on."

"No one's trying to do anything," Mom said softly, conciliatorily. It was her make-everything-all-right voice. It didn't work very well lately. "Nothing's going on, Malcolm. These are your friends."

"They're not. You've changed them. They want to hurt me. Everything's changed."

Aunty was getting angry. She was taking the drinks out of people's hands now, hissing, *"Party's over!"* People were getting angry back too. Mom took a couple of steps toward Dad, which seemed to frighten him even more. He put his hands up in front of himself, his body rigidly poised for defense. Then he stepped forward and Mom stepped back. The crowd was thinning. Foster could hear Aunty shepherding the last of the guests out to their cars.

He was thinking about climbing out his window and making his way back in through the front door. He felt oddly vulnerable as a bookend to Dad's increasing fear. That was when Mom said, "Close your door, Fossie."

Dad immediately spun around with his arms still raised and gasped, his face twisted with the shock of discovering someone behind him. Foster skidded backward into his room, his arms windmilling to maintain balance. Dad's expression was dragged like a mad cat through alarm, then panic, then rage in the few seconds that hovered un-moving in the thickened air. Then he turned and bolted for the bathroom.

Foster ran out of his room and would have thrown himself at Mom had she not countered with a side step, heading toward the bathroom door herself. She moved so fast that Foster tripped slightly, forced into a running stop when his velocity wasn't halted by Mom's firm grasp. Foster could see out the open front door now. Aunty was shoving Blinky into the back of his parents' car. Foster thought it looked like a shove, anyway, and when she turned around, even from this distance, Foster could see the party wreckage on her face. She was striding back to the house with arms pumping while Blinky's dad was still talking at her. She was just a few steps from the front door when the sound of shattering glass ricocheted down the hall. Foster let out a yelp at the shock, which was quickly followed by a long and distressed scream from the bathroom.

Aunty was running by the time she made it to the hallway. She clipped Foster on the way past, but she kept going. Foster was really irritated by now. On top of being plain frightened by the chaos, he was having trouble staying on his feet. Foster watched, appalled, as Mom pounded on the bathroom door, begging Dad to unlock it. Dad was screaming, stopping only to bemoan the stranger in the bathroom with him and the blood.

"Blood? There's blood?" Aunty called to him through the door. Then she said to Mom, "I'm calling an ambulance."

"Who's in there with you?" Mom was calling. "Hello? Hello? Please open the door!"

"No one's in there with him," Aunty said. Then she was giving their address to someone on the phone.

Foster was mesmerized. Every one of his senses was tingling, and yet he felt strangely detached. He couldn't seem to move his deadened limbs, but his skin was crawling and his chest was alight. He felt he had to move to survive this. The front door was right there, still open. He knew he had to run, but he couldn't. Then he had the loneliest thought he had ever had: He would stand here, unseen and unheard, and be consumed by this havoc inside him as surely as Grandma had been consumed by dragon fire. He would likely die of it.

The noises were terrible. Everyone's noises were terrible. The ambulance siren, which at first hovered like distant smoke and then became as loud as a kick in the head, did nothing to induce the calming relief of help being on the way. It was when the siren shut off in the driveway, and they were all slapped by the sudden silencing of it, that a moment of quiet landed. But it didn't last long.

The ambulance men rushed in. Foster thought they looked like soldiers. He hadn't noticed before, but Mom was on her knees trying to pick the lock on the bathroom door with a knife. She stood suddenly, sweaty and panting, the knife pointed directly at the ambulance man in front of her, and said, "I think he might have hurt himself."

"Why don't you go and look after the young one," he said, easing the knife from Mom's shaking hand. Aunty grabbed her arm then and pulled her away.

The men shouldered the bathroom door open. Foster had only ever seen that done in the movies. It wasn't as easy as it looked in the movies either. It took several tries, and when it finally gave way, the doorframe cracked like a lightning strike.

The men were in the bathroom with Dad for a while. He yelled at them a lot, but they kept talking in quiet, calm voices. Dad was getting tired. Mom was crying. Aunty was leaning against the wall. Eventually one of the ambulance men went and got a gurney, and they helped Dad climb onto it and then strapped him down. Foster could see bandages on Dad's hands and there was blood on his clothes.

As they wheeled Dad down the hall and toward the front door, Foster backed up until he was on the veranda. That was when he noticed how many people were out on the street. Some of the party guests hadn't left at all. They were still sitting in their cars waiting and watching. Miss Watson was on the sidewalk. Foster waited to feel humiliated, or angry, or protective. He waited to feel something. He watched Dad being loaded into the ambulance and realized the dead in his limbs had crawled through his entire body and snatched his heart. He would have to feel about this later.

Blood
and Glass

Mom went with Dad in the ambulance. Aunty stayed behind with Foster, who had to be coaxed back into the house from his rigid position on the veranda. Cars and people began to leave once the ambulance had left. It had left quietly, sirens and lights dormant. Foster knew that meant Dad was going to be okay. They weren't planning on running any traffic lights to speed up the journey to the hospital. Foster had seen ambulances do that, and had been in the car with Mom when she'd mounted a sidewalk to get out of the way of a wailing ambulance. She'd said that meant the person inside was very, very sick. But Foster's relief at the lack of a loud, flashy-light departure immediately disappeared when he saw the bathroom.

He didn't know how long he had been standing in the hallway. He didn't even remember Aunty closing the front door. But by the time he wheeled his limbs into motion and made his way down the hall, Aunty was already in the bathroom cleaning up.

The bathroom mirror was broken. A few pieces were still attached to the frame, sharp and sinister as monster teeth, but the rest were scattered on the tiles, some bejeweled with tremulous baubles of bright blood. There was blood on the walls and on the side of the bathtub, and more on the floor and on the underside of the sink. Aunty was carefully lifting the pieces of mirror and laying them onto sheets of newspaper, some of which had become soaked at the edges. She looked up at Foster, her fingertips slick, and said, "Oh, Fossie, I thought you were in your room. Don't watch this."

"Is that Dad's blood?"

Aunty began folding the edges of the newspaper together, wrapping the glass as carefully as Foster had wrapped *The General*.

"Don't worry," she said. "All he did was cut his hands a bit."

"Why?"

"Because the glass is sharp."

"No, I mean why did the mirror break?"

"I . . . I'm not sure."

"Did Dad break the mirror? Is that how he cut his hands?"

"I think so."

"Why did Dad break the mirror?"

"Fossie, please. Go and find something to do and we'll talk about this later."

"You have blood on you."

"Fossie! *Please!*"

Aunty heaved the words at Foster unexpectedly loudly. He could hear the pieces of mirror chinking about in the newspaper parcel Aunty was making. He didn't go and find something to do, though. What was he supposed to do? He had just discovered that a room spattered with blood has a rusty smell that clears out the senses and coats the tongue. He didn't think he could play right now.

"Get me a plastic bag from the kitchen, Fossie?"

He was going to. He could see himself walking in there, opening that bottom drawer, pulling out a squeaky bag or two, returning to the bathroom. But he hadn't moved. He realized he hadn't moved when there was a firm knock at the front door. In his head he was holding plastic bags for Aunty. In his body he was empty-handed, being knocked on as surely as if he were a door.

"For goodness' sake," Aunty muttered. Then she looked up and said, "Foster, get me a plastic bag!"

"Are you going to answer the door?"

"No."

Foster was walking to the kitchen for real this time when the knock on the door happened again. He didn't think about it. He just opened the door. It was the normal thing to do.

Miss Watson was wringing her hands in a way that gave Foster goose bumps. She looked down at him, then past him down the hall, before saying, "Go and get your mom."

"She's not here."

"You're not home alone?"

"No, he's not," Aunty said, walking up behind Foster. "Can I help you, Myra?"

"I came to see if I could help you," Miss Watson said.

"Thank you. No."

"Is that blood?"

Foster turned around to see what Miss Watson was seeing. Aunty was looking down at her shirt and her hands. But the blood was on one knee of her jeans. Perhaps she hadn't noticed. Perhaps she hadn't heard Foster when he told her about it. So he pointed to it. "There," he said.

"Is someone hurt?" Miss Watson asked.

"No," Aunty replied.

"Yes," Foster said. He felt Aunty's fingers grip his shoulder, just like the old lady's church grip. He didn't care. "Dad broke a mirror and cut himself. There was blood *everywhere*. Aunty and I are cleaning it up."

"Not really a job for a child," Miss Watson said to Aunty.

"What do you want, Myra?"

"What do you want, Myra?" Foster hadn't known he was going to repeat it until the words were out of his mouth. Miss Watson looked shocked. It felt good to him. Aunty squeezed his shoulder more firmly.

"Cheeky!" Miss Watson said.

"Cheeky," Foster repeated.

"Fossie, stop it!" Aunty demanded.

Foster turned and looked at Aunty and said, "Fossie, stop it," straight back at her, but without the distress he could plainly feel in her grip and tone.

"Myra, I have to go," Aunty said, pulling Foster back from the open door.

"There's something wrong with that child," Miss Watson said as the door swung closed.

"There's something wrong with that child," Foster said. Aunty leaned her back against the front door, her hands on her hips.

"Plastic bag?" she said.

Foster stood for a long time in front of the mirror in his bedroom. It was the only one that hadn't been turned to the wall. So far. The big mirror with the fancy frame in the family room had been taken down. The small one in the hall that Mom used to check her face before going out had been turned around. That had been easy to do, because it hung on a little chain. The miniature cheval mirror Dad had bought Mom as a birthday gift had been tucked in the bottom of her wardrobe with her shoes. She had another long one in their bedroom that was bolted to the wall. That had been covered with a sheet that draped in long, stiff meringues of shiny cotton, ghostlike. It bothered Foster even when he wasn't looking at it. He just had to imagine it. Foster thought there was something unpleasant, wrong even, in covering mirrors. Rooms looked darker, unlived in. It was like putting away pieces of Dad himself.

A boy at school had said that when his granddad died, they had to cover all the mirrors in the house in case his granddad's soul got trapped in one and couldn't get to heaven. Foster had said that was stupid. But now he felt nervous and helpless watching Mom treating mirrors as if Dad were dead.

So he stood in front of the mirror in his bedroom, which he was allowed to do as long as he covered it with a tea towel afterward in case Dad went in there. He tried to imagine seeing a stranger there instead of his own reflection. He squeezed his eyes shut for so long that when he opened them, he had to rapid-blink his face into focus, but it was still and always his own face. He turned his back to the mirror and spun around to see if some other person peeked out of the mirror while he wasn't looking. It didn't matter what he did—he only ever saw himself. He even touched the mirror, something Mom hated because they were so difficult to polish. He wondered how hard Dad had had to punch the stranger he saw to shatter the cold, hard surface. He liked the way the mirror felt, and Mom wasn't likely to be polishing the mirrors now anyway.

Everyone said it was a mistake—that Dad just hadn't recognized himself and that this was a part of his illness. When he thought he saw a stranger in the mirror, he'd been frightened. Foster heard them all talking about it when Dad came home from the hospital. James was there, and Aunty, and another person he hadn't seen before. It was this other person, a chubby woman, who suggested covering or removing the mirrors. Mom had made some tea and they were all sitting at the kitchen table, including Dad.

"If Dad punched the mirror because he thought it was a stranger, why isn't he punching you?" Foster asked Chubby Lady.

Everyone looked at him. His voice seemed to have the ability to startle people lately. It was powerful to be forgotten.

"That's inappropriate, Fossie. Apologize," Mom said. Aunty was smiling, though. Chubby Lady leaned forward.

"He's not frightened right now. And he knows I'm here to help," she said.

"How do you know he knows that?" Foster asked.

"Well, he's quite happy, isn't he?"

"He's doing his imaginary sewing. He does that when he's not happy," Foster said.

"That's enough, Foster," Mom said, reflexively resting her hands on Dad's to still their busyness.

Chubby Lady continued talking to Mom. "You may find the worst time of day in terms of distress is late afternoon. We're not really sure why. It's fairly common, though. 'Sundowning,' they call it, and there are—"

"I think he was scrying," Foster said.

"You think he was crying?" James asked.

"Scrying! Dad told me about it. Mirrors are magic. Dad told me a story about Nostril Dumbass who lived hundreds of years ago. He used mirrors and bowls of water to see into the future. And other people did too. Witches and queens like the one in *Snow White*. That's why we shouldn't cover the mirrors, because Dad was scrying. We need to know what he saw. Has anyone just asked him what he *saw?*"

Everyone was looking at him. Foster swallowed hard to push his heart back down to where it was supposed to be. "People did it before they went into battle, even! Just to decide what to do about stuff and find out what other people were doing, and if you had some dragon's blood—"

"Enough!" Mom shouted. She wasn't usually a shouty person, but Foster had noticed that lately she wore the kind of sour face that smacked of a whole lot of stuff rolling around just beneath the surface. It was the sort of face Dad would say was begging for a good scrying. Foster had also noticed that most of the time she spoke to him lately, it involved her being spitty and him being humiliated. He didn't like being shouted at, especially in front of strangers who should be punched, not invited to the table to talk about Dad as if he weren't even in the room.

Foster knew that breaking the mirror proved that the general was still in there. That he still had his great powers. No one else understood, and he couldn't make them understand if they all looked at him like they'd been slapped upside the head by a wet fish and then became shouty. There was no cavalry in that room. The clothespin basket was getting tighter and tighter around the captive. Foster could almost see the imprint of its hard plastic edges on Dad's face. That snarl of lines around his eyes was his skintight prison getting close enough to choke him.

No one said anything for a while. There was just tea-sipping and contemplation. When James reached across and took hold of Foster's hand under the table, Foster slapped it away because that one act of kindness might make him go bonkers.

"I think we need to talk about all these things you're worried about, Foster," James said. "But probably not now. A bit later."

"I'm not worried," Foster said.

"Have you thought about getting some help for the boy?" Chubby Lady said this while leaning across the table to touch the back of Mom's hand. The touch made Mom raise her eyes and look directly at Foster. "We can help organize some counseling for him. He seems slightly detached from reality. There are support programs for the children of—"

Foster hadn't climbed the jacaranda in a long time. He began to feel the familiar flurry of tickly, papery wings in his chest that always made him want to climb. But it was dark outside, and there was a moon tonight. It had risen into the top left corner of the kitchen window and glazed everything nicely. Foster liked the moon. He liked its predictable changing from nothing to fullness. He liked the way its light was put out every month and then came back. He knew it was called waxing and waning. Dad had told him that. Dad had even sung him a song about it. Foster tried to remember the words to the song now but the only thing he could keep in his head was the song about a bullfrog named Jeremiah. So he sang that instead.

Tender
Meat

"**W**hat are you thinking about?"

Mom had been asking Foster this quite a lot lately. Dad used to ask him that too. But Mom asked it differently from Dad. She asked as if she had no real curiosity. She asked as if she had been told to ask him because asking would show interest. She was never looking at him when she asked. She was always busy with something else, her hands and eyes constantly moving. If there had been a stillness to the question, Foster might have welcomed it. But he had an awful feeling that Mom wanting in on his thoughts was just a trap he'd better not step into. Saying what he thought hadn't gone too well for him lately. His shift from the ancient tradition of using frogs and toads in magic to "Jeremiah was a bullfrog" had made Mom burst into tears and earned him an appointment with a special doctor who also spent most of the time asking Foster what he was thinking about. So, rather than feel relieved that he was being seen and his thoughts were valued, Foster just felt bossed around.

When Mom asked "What are you thinking about?" her face said she was far, far away. Maybe even back in her castle. Mostly Mom seemed tired. The strange thing was that it wasn't a normal tired. It didn't look like the kind of tired that follows hard work or a long time concentrating on something important. Mom didn't roll her shoulders or yawn or get up to put the kettle on like she usually did when she was feeling tired. This was a moody tired. It made her unpredictable, and Foster heard her complaining to Aunty on the phone about headaches. Her words became a bit slurred, and she seemed to cry more easily than she used to.

A couple of times, Foster came across Mom with her head drooped, rivulets of drool greasing her chin. He learned quickly enough that she was not comfortably napping and she might swing from this inactivity to anger without warning and with even less grace. Whenever Foster came across her in this state of dozy instability, he played quietly and watched the clock, waiting for Dad to come home.

Dad was spending more time during weekends at day care. When Dad was in the house, Foster felt a single purpose. To tell him stories, read him picture books, and watch his face. Foster was sure that even if Dad wasn't talking, he was listening, so he behaved as if rescue was always imminent.

Dad was always more responsive after day care. Foster felt it was a shame that Mom seemed to miss out on Dad's best hour because she was already very tired when he got home. Aunty usually drove Dad home from day care because Mom had already had a few tired wines. Foster reckoned that probably helped her when Dad wasn't very nice to her. It certainly helped her not bite back, which everyone said she absolutely must not do. But then one day Mom had bitten back in a way that shocked everyone.

That particular afternoon, Dad was really chatty. They were all gathered around the kitchen table apart from Mom, who, after checking that Geraldine was still in the yard, started peeling beets at the sink. Aunty encouraged Foster and Mom to join in, to try to be involved in the stories Dad was remembering, even if he didn't seem to be making much sense. Foster was happy to sit holding Dad's hand while Aunty tried to steer him toward things that had happened a long time ago. That was his best place, his happiest place. The long ago. So between all the hissing and harrumphing Dad sprayed in Mom's direction, he had periods of nonstop banter and giggling with Aunty and Foster. It reminded Foster of that Christmas when Dad had had four glasses of blueberry port with a beer chaser. There was the same joyous temper in his tone and his eyes. Every now and then he would bawl at Mom for a few seconds, his irritation increasing when Mom didn't respond. But Aunty would bring him back to point with a distraction, a question, a memory.

Foster didn't notice that Dad had become quiet right away. He was watching Mom deliberately doing the lazy peel on the beets. She said beet peeling had to be done quickly and efficiently to prevent skin staining. Foster had always liked watching her do it. But this time she was doing it slowly, haphazardly rolling the bulbs in her palms, deliberately smearing herself with the purple juice. It bothered him in the same way it bothered him when Mum dressed Dad in clothes that didn't match. He was about to walk over to her and ask if he could help when he noticed Dad staring at her in a peculiar way. Then Dad said, "The gall of that woman."

He actually used that word too. *Gall*. Foster remembered that very clearly because he had thought Gall was an ancient Roman province. He had only recently read about it in a picture book.

Aunty immediately interceded, "Malcolm, do you remember that dog we had when we were kids? The one that went missing for weeks and we all thought we'd never see again? Even put up a memorial to it in the back garden. And then it just walked into the yard one day! Do you remember that? You loved that dog so much. Dad let him sleep on your bed after that because you were so worried he'd go missing again. What was that dog's name? Do you remember that dog?"

"Geraldine?"

"Geraldine's the dog we have now, Dad."

"Oh." Dad paused, seemed to go away for a bit, and then said, "People in Korea eat dogs. In soups and stews. The best meat is from a beaten dog. Makes the meat tender. They say a beaten dog tastes better."

That was when Mom reacted. She bristled quite noticeably, as if she had a bad taste in her mouth or someone had walked on her grave. She turned slowly to look at them and then filled her cheeks with air. Foster looked again and more closely, just to make sure, but that was exactly what she was doing: puffing out her cheeks until they were all mottled, her eyes squeezed shut. He wondered if she would burst. He wondered if her cheeks were full of words, trapped in there behind her teeth. Foster imagined those trapped words milling about, trying to knit themselves into proper-meaning things. He suddenly felt nervous. He pressed his lips together to prevent a smile from splitting his face. Then Mom pressed both her hands down on the kitchen table, palms flat and fingers extended. She leaned forward, simultaneously releasing all the air in her face. The hot rush that was discharged from Mom's pooched lips made a squeaky fart noise and was close enough to Dad to disturb his hair. Then Mom said the only word that had been stuck in there. "Woof."

Dad stood up and released a *yawp* that shuddered through the house. Foster scooted out of his chair and pressed himself against the wall. Safest place to be. He didn't know why, but it occurred to him that that was precisely the sort of noise one would make just before throwing something. He had never heard Dad make a sound like that before. He didn't know anything that deep and gravelly could come out of a person. Aunty began fussing with dishes and talking loud and fast at everyone and no one, thrusting plates with uncharacteristic force into the sink. Foster wondered if he should help her clean up, but there was something in her manner that made this look like more than just a cleaning-up. Aunty looked like she was preparing to clear out. If she was, Foster decided, he was going with her. Mom uprighted herself and stepped away from the table, leaving two purple handprints as dark as bruises. She looked very heavy-lidded and steely angry. Her face made Foster ache in a strange way. It was more than fear making Foster's chest thump and mouth dry out. It was awe. Mom had managed to slap them all down with one hot word.

March

Hares

Things were weird. All the grown-ups in the house had started looking at each other sideways.

Aunty had moved in with her dog, Archie, which Dad took to with an affection that baffled Foster, given Geraldine was still in danger of being pushed into oncoming traffic by the very same man. Mom complained about the dog being in the house all the time. She said it stank. She had a brief and triumphant hissy fit when she started finding what she thought was dog poo all over the house. Finding out that Dad was collecting his own poo in ice-cream containers seemed only to disappoint her, because then she didn't have an excuse to throw the dog out. Other than that, Mom seemed to take all these changes in stride. Foster watched her seeking out suspicious containers hidden around the house.

Mom worked more hours because Aunty was able to be there in the evenings. Foster felt better with Aunty there. Even though Mom and Aunty still weren't good friends, Aunty was a good buffer between Dad and Mom. Dad didn't get anywhere near as angry at Aunty as he did at Mom.

There had been a meeting after the woofing business. That was what Aunty called it. *The woofing business.* Foster didn't understand why Mom had woofed at Dad, only that something had changed that day. Something had broken. Like when mountain goats perch their twiggy-legged bodies on rock faces and then suddenly head butt each other off. Foster had seen it on a TV show. Dad said they have cloven hooves that help them keep their balance on very small ledges. They look impossibly stable on the steepest cliffs. But even the most sure-footed can topple, especially when challenged by another goat. Whenever something went really wrong, Dad would always laugh and say "Well, she's at the bottom of the mountain now." Just like a head-butted goat. That was how Foster felt. No more pretending to balance. No more pretending at all.

"I think it's really important that we're all honest with each other here," James said. Aunty had organized the meeting because she thought Mom was "losing her marbles." That was what she had said on the phone, anyway. So James, Sophie, Skinny Lady, Mom, and Aunty all sat in the family room with no tea tray and no sausage rolls. Mom couldn't be bothered, apparently, to which Aunty had said, "Thank God!" Dad was in day care. Foster sat in the kitchen with his soldiers.

"She's at the bottom of the mountain now," Foster said loudly.

"Fossie, what are you doing in there?" Mom asked.

"Eavesdropping."

"How do you know a word like that?" Sophie asked.

"From Dad."

"What did you mean, Foster? What did you mean when you said '*She's at the bottom of the mountain now*'?" James asked.

"It's something Dad would say when someone lost their marbles."

There was a brief silence before Aunty started to laugh, something she attempted to swallow in a discreet snicker but that eventually cracked the air in a great barking guffaw. Soon she was gulp-sighing on the exhale and snot-sniffing on the inhale.

"That's so true!" she said.

"What else did your dad say?" Sophie asked.

"He said that stories are the most important thing. He said people don't tell stories or listen to other people's stories enough. He said people are mad as March hares but to love them anyway. He said battles are won or lost before the first shot is fired. He said babies need to get the finger of God on them. He said if God is real, then so are dragons. He said the brain is a superhero and he said Mom is a princess. Oh, and he said an unkind word can clear a room quicker than a fart."

All of this was delivered while Foster moved his soldiers around the spill-stained placemat in front of him. He used cutlery to make a shining river through the brown wasteland and contemplated a full-frontal desperado assault over the benefits of a guerrilla-pincer move. A few moments passed before he realized everyone had gone silent. He wondered if they'd all snuck out of the house like Dad sometimes did. He looked over and could see heads above the top of the couch. He waited a bit longer, then slid from his chair and walked over.

"Why are you crying, Mom?"

"Tired, Fossie. Just tired."

"Do you want some wine, then?"

"Just come sit with me."

Mom scooched over in Dad's lounge chair so Foster would have enough room to squeeze in. He liked that.

"Well. Now that we're all at the bottom of the mountain together," Sophie said, "let's get a plan in place that suits everyone and make sure everyone gets the support they need. Carer burnout is a serious and devastating issue, and we are on the cusp of that here. So let's just open the floor and . . ."

Foster unfurled his fingers and wiped his palm sweat

off the general with the bottom of his shirt. Mom's hand rested on the small of his back, making circular motions like she used to do to coax him to sleep when he was little. The general had started looking rough. His sword was gone, snapped off when Foster had accidentally stepped on him. The small disk of plastic grass he was rooted to had cracked. Still solid enough to keep him on his feet, but something needed to be done about it. Foster wasn't allowed to use the smelly glue because it could stick your fingers together so bad you'd need a blowtorch to get them apart again. At least, that was what Dad said. But some sticky tape would work in a pinch. One of the general's eyebrows had rubbed off too. Foster thought he should stop picking him up by the head.

It took a while to get used to the door alarms. In the beginning everyone other than Dad started setting them off. They weren't scary alarms. They played songs or chimed, depending on which door it was and whether it was being opened or closed. Foster would just call out "Sorry, that was me!" and Mom or Aunty would come and reset it. When Aunty set one off, she would usually mutter a bad word and reset it herself. Eventually they got used to the alarms. They didn't frighten Dad, which was the main thing.

James said it was important to keep Dad and everyone else in the house safe. Special clips were put on the cupboard doors. Foster could still open the cupboards. It was just fiddly work. You had to slide your fingers inside a gap and push on a plastic spring. There was nothing in those cupboards Foster needed, but he couldn't help trying out the little clips to see how difficult they really were.

Dad never attempted to snake his fingers inside the small opening. He seemed happily resigned to a drawer not opening when he pulled on it. Mom left two cabinets unclipped and filled them with plastic bowls and lids so that Dad could pull everything out and put everything back in if he felt like it. Sometimes Foster would help him sort out the right lid for each container.

Mom removed the door locks on the bathroom and bedroom doors too—just in case. Foster didn't like that so much. He couldn't reach the bathroom door while he was sitting on the toilet, and Dad kept walking in on him. That meant Foster had to call out for Mom or Aunty to come and get Dad. That meant even more people fussing about in the bathroom while he sat there with his tighty-whities around his ankles. Foster started holding it and only pooing at school.

They went for walks in the late afternoon—when the sun was going down in both the day and Dad. That restless time of day when Dad became unsettled and sometimes even angry. Foster liked the walks best if it had been raining, if there were puddles reflecting the last of the light, making even the smallest water slick on the path look like an entire world. Dad said there were worlds everywhere if you looked for them. They'd take Archie on the walks. Dad liked to hold the leash. As they walked, Dad's face would begin to settle, his fingers would begin to rest, and he would start to talk. Mom would link arms with him on the leash side and Foster would hold his other hand. When they got home, Dad would seem more rested and Aunty would use the opportunity to take Geraldine for a walk. Sometimes Foster would go with her because he felt sorry for Geraldine. They couldn't walk both dogs together. It made Dad angry.

The walks weren't always a good thing. Sometimes they'd get to the end of the garden path and have to grapple with Dad to get him turned around and right back inside again. Aunty would say "Never mind" and put some music on instead. Aunty said if you can get used to the idea that the routine isn't always routine, then you'll never be kicked in the rear by your own expectations. Foster wasn't sure exactly what that meant, because a routine was routine, but it made Mom laugh, so he did too.

They went for drives. They didn't necessarily get out of the car when they got to where they were going. It was always dependent on Dad. Foster liked the drives because Dad would hum. Dad used to hum a lot when he drove the car. Foster would close his eyes and imagine it was Dad driving with Mom in the passenger seat like it always had been. And maybe they would stop for ice cream.

Dad usually enjoyed the car ride to pick up Foster from school, but this particular afternoon when Foster climbed into the backseat, he could tell that Dad was angry and

Mom was clearly close to losing her marbles again. Aunty must have been at work, because Mom wouldn't usually make Dad get in the car in this mood if there was someone she could leave him with at home.

"Let me out," Dad said. "Let me out now. I know what you're doing. Let me out!" He pulled on the door handle and slapped the car window.

"It's all right, Malcolm. We're going home now."

"Why are you doing this to me?" Dad said. Mom pulled onto the street and put her foot down. She was in a hurry. Foster had told her he could walk home. It wasn't far at all. But she said it wasn't safe. Foster wasn't feeling particularly safe right now, especially when Dad swung his arm wide and slapped a stinging blow on Mom's upper arm. She pulled the car so suddenly into the curb that the front tire skidded against the concrete and Dad hit his head on the side window. They just sat there then. Engine running, Mom breathing hard, Dad still doing battle with the car door. Foster could see Dad's hands through the little gap between the front passenger seat and the door. His fingers were grasping, scratching, prying, as if he were being covered in dirt and trying to punch a hole through to the sky. It frightened Foster terribly.

"Foster, how are you doing back there?" Mom asked, her head resting on the steering wheel. "I didn't bring anything for his hands. I'm sorry."

They were supposed to do that. They were supposed to always have a distraction ready. That was when Foster remembered he had one.

He quickly unzipped his backpack and pulled it out. He had been carrying it around with him since the birthday party. His hands were shaking. The wrapping had taken a bit of a beating. The corners were worn and the shiny red paper was scuffed and scratched. He removed his seat belt and leaned forward, poking it through that little gap until it rested on the back of one of Dad's shimmying hands.

"Dad, I have a present for you," Foster said.

Dad took hold of the bright red package immediately. Foster slid toward the middle of the backseat and leaned forward to watch Dad turning the present this way and that, running his hands across the paper. Mom looked on for a moment, then reached over and picked at the edge of a piece of sticky tape. It was enough to encourage Dad to start picking at it as well, and then eventually start tearing the paper away altogether.

Foster hadn't seen it in so long himself that he had forgotten just how good the cover was. Dad opened the book, lifted it to his face, and smelled it. He always did that with new books.

"It's beautiful, Foster," Mom said. She said to Dad, "Foster made that."

"I wrote it too," Foster said.

"The General," Dad read. "It's lovely. Look at the pictures."

"Let's go home and read it," Mom said.

"Let's read it now," Dad said.

Foster saw Mom hesitate. They were stopped outside
someone else's house with the car running, and they were
so close to home. They could see their street sign from
here.

"Look, I think—"

"Once upon a time . . . ," Foster began.

Mom turned the engine off.

Routine isn't always routine. Foster reckoned sometimes it's just better to crawl under the overturned
clothespin basket yourself.

Acknowledgments

I would like to thank everyone at Allen & Unwin, particularly Erica Wagner for her guidance and support from the onset. Thanks also to Angela Namoi for tirelessly spreading the word and to Sophie Splatt, because editing me can't be one of the fun jobs.

I would also like to thank Kate Sullivan at Penguin Random House for reading and editing so sensitively.

My love and thanks always to Linda Brooks, Ainslie Douglas, and Jenny McDonald, who have supported me during a year they were barely able to stand themselves.

And to Robert Schofield for his invaluable insight into the first draft and for always having the breath of kindness.

About the Author

Dianne Touchell was born and raised in Fremantle, Western Australia. Her debut novel, *Creepy & Maud,* was shortlisted for the Children's Book Council of Australia's Book of the Year Award in the Older Readers category. She has worked as a fry cook, a nightclub singer, a housekeeper, a bookseller, and a manager of a construction company. Sometimes she has time to write books for young adults, who she thinks are far more interesting than grown-ups. She lives with animals.